Elizabeth Ashworth has worked as a journalist and
taught in Sicily and Greece. She now lives in north
Wales, where she teaches, writes and paints. Her
poems, journalism, paintings and short stories have
all won prizes. This is her first published novel.

T0149088

PARTHIAN BOOKS

So I kissed her little sister

Elizabeth Ashworth

PARTHIAN BOOKS

Parthian Books
53 Colum Road
Cardiff
CF1 3EF

First published in 1999.
All rights reserved.
© Elizabeth Ashworth
ISBN 1-902638-02-6

This book is published through **The Cambrensis Initiative,** which is a programme of publication supported by an Arts for All grant from the Arts Council of Wales.

Parthian would like to thank the Lottery Unit and the people who make it possible for the direct support of the Cambrensis Initiative.

Typeset in Galliard by NW.

Printed and bound by ColourBooks, Dublin 13, Ireland.

With support from the Parthian Collective.

A CIP catalogue record for this book is available from the British Library.

The author wishes to acknowledge the award of a bursary from the Arts Council of Wales, for the purpose of writing this book.

For my family and friends

With thanks to Joel, Jane and Mike,
Lewis Davies and Stevie Davies -
and to Pat, for being in the pram with me

Took she ducklings to the water
Every morning just at nine
Hit her foot against a splinter
Fell into the foaming brine

O, my darling, O, my darling
O, my darling Clementine
You are lost and gone for ever
Dreadful sorry, Clementine.

Ruby lips above the water
Blowing bubbles mighty fine
But alas, I was no swimmer
So I lost my Clementine

How I missed her, how I missed her
How I missed my Clementine
So I kissed her little sister
And forgot my Clementine

DAY ONE THOUSAND

"Relationships, is it?" she asks, when she first sits down.

"I might have killed her."

"And is that your first memory?"

It isn't: but while I'm on the subject, all the long-forgotten details of that scene come flooding back vividly: the oblong kitchen windows, their panes covered inside with flimsy stained-glass paper, peeling at the corners; the big black pram standing underneath, speckled with red, blue and yellow lights; inside my gurgling little sister, with her tuft of pale brown hair; my mam ironing. She had three sizes of flat-iron which she heated on the gas ring, then lifted up so that she could spit on their shiny bottoms, and the saliva rolled sputtering away.

And me, rocking my sister in the black pram, but so hard that Lottie nearly fell out, and while mam rescued her and shouted at me, my dad jumped up and told her I hadn't meant it. I was the apple of his eye: he had always been my champion.

"But things had begun to change with the advent of your sister?"

"I felt there must have been something bad about me, I suppose. No one had said a new baby was expected, and then, as soon as she arrived, I was sent to school."

"At two and a half?"

"This was 1945, remember, and that sort of thing was usual, when the primary school was so near."

"It didn't mean they didn't love you, though."

"Yes, I know. Everything was fine, really - until art college."

"Because you felt diminished?"

It is clearer in my mind, now: I am walking to school, and it is surely with my mother, along the back alley, behind the ground floor flat of the house where we live. I see that shaded wall, on my right, with lichened, impassive stones, whose presence insists on my solitary fate. Dusty cobwebs here and there I rub off with my trailing, childish palm, until we come through the tall iron gate and onto a patch of scrubby land, where I am vanquished in the young sunshine, but squint still at ladybirds in nettles, and feign innocent joy beneath the blue void of morning.

At four, I am writing in my exercise book with a nibbed pen, dipped in blue ink from a white pot in the wooden desk: I read to the school inspector, standing on a chair in front of the class; blushing, articulate, melancholy, freakish.

I tell Mary how I drew and painted for hours in solitude.

"But I was good at sums, and as I got older, I set myself long divisions for fun - the longer, the better! I liked seeing how far I could take them. I loved spelling, too - trying out words like 'rhododendron' and 'miscellaneous' inside my book of *The Flower Fairies*."

I describe to her how, sometimes, my dad would take my hand, and the two of us would walk home from a pantomime in starlight, or stroll on a windblown golf course in spring. But by now I was a dreamer, playing princes and princesses by myself, piling up my dolls in the eiderdown, in games of loss and disappointment.

"So the world of the imagination, and being precocious and creative, was beginning to be bound up with the sense of being an outcast?"

Farther back still, I continue - the real first memory: my dark-haired mother, standing in the doorway of the nursing home, with the newborn sister in her arms, wrapped in a big white shawl. We'd gone to fetch them in George's taxi, and I sat looking out of the back window while my dad collected them.

Mary watches me, intent, with concerned brown eyes over her file.

"And seeing them from the car you felt separated from your

mother and father, and all alone for the first time in your life ?"

"Maybe. Then my dad started to sing 'Clementine' at bedtime - and that line stuck in my mind: 'So I kissed her little sister... and forgot my Clementine.'"

Mary gazes round the room, thoughtfully, as my eyes brim with tears of self-pity at the trauma to the impressionable, if robust, infant in the back of the taxi. She admires my vase of silk roses, and says my cottage is charming: that I should concentrate on these talents of mine for painting and writing, and make a good life for myself, now I'm thinking of resigning from the job.

I like Mary: she seems sane, optimistic and compassionate, and is doing her best to understand what is the matter. She has been allocated to me because my female GP thinks that I need help. I've had a chest infection which has left me weak and depressed, and, as the weeks have gone by, I've found myself less able to face returning to work. I've had some tests for anaemia, amid lots of erratic speeches and weeping in the surgery, and now the doctor has signed me off for a month, and sent Mary.

But I can't imagine never going back: even though the job has almost overwhelmed me with its relentless demands, I'm nourished by its unhealthy distractions, and also have no financial choice but to stay with it.

Four years ago, I had welcomed the chance to be a reporter on the local paper, seeing it as a real and distinguished new beginning, after years of teaching, or careworn little earners.

"Put that typewriter away and use the computer," the editor snapped at me, on the heels of my twenty-minute training session on the first day. Nervous and embarrassed, I mumbled that I would, in a minute, continuing to type, as on The Dead Sea Scrolls, that Ziggy would be on keyboards with 'Owzat!' at the Usher Inn.

Each day, in the smoke and sweat-polluted office of the *North-West Messenger,* I tapped away scrupulously on 'Pubtalk' in the corner, ringing round the local taverns to see what entertainment they were laying on. Since the initial notes I'd made on how to use the word-processor, every working moment had become a leap through one or another flaming hoop. I looked at good literature on the bus in the morning, to find a way of beginning sentences in an interesting way - but was soon to discover, as far as the *Messenger* was concerned, the potency of the ubiquitous 'and' in every news story:

'And Mrs Ramsbottom is staging a sit-in at the store.'

'And locals are up in arms.'

'And police say they are baffled.'

Bible copies of the newspaper slithered yellowly from their piles behind the place where I spun on my seedy moquette chair. The born-again Christian librarian asked if he could ply me with hot chocolate; a pre-Raphaelite girl typed and gazed, rapt at her screen. Telephones rang; sixteen people swivelled and swore while passing messages under noses; the courier, a frogman, puffing and panting, stomped through in his motorbike helmet and his leathers, a dewdrop forever hanging from his nostril and his specs forever misted over. His presence, as he hovered at my desk, snorted urgency, deadlines, Reuter and speeding fines, while he grabbed envelopes of films for processing, or delivered letters, books, press releases and Red Arrow parcels. Then, mid-morning, the trolley appeared, and there stood Molly, in her perm and overall, creating the illusion of oasis, with her largesse of crisps and KitKats, and we drank tea or coffee, and talked further on the phone; each in his or her own world. It was perfect.

To start with, and for the first two years, I was happy - even while I sat at council meetings in wet Welsh towns, in cold rooms lit by neon and warmed by a one-bar fire, where mayors and clerks strutted their hour; where the fate of many a string of bunting hung in the balance; where deputations of anoraked locals straight after tea and no messing scented and flavoured the fetid air with fish fingers and invective.

After training in shorthand, politics and government, I could get the quotes in a flash in my Teeline, and, by now, I knew the law. With one loaded phone call, dangerous old buildings were demolished, and eyesore tunnel entrances grassed and daisied; the inoperable were cured; the embarrassed received finance. Villagers brought me their triumphs and tragedies; over a pint I uncovered a dirty doing here or an unsung hero there; I was their agent for action; scribe to scores of scallywags.

I interviewed, produced volumes of copy, stayed late into the evening, got drunk, hallucinated. I never stopped talking and I was never without an idea. Thanks to the MOD and St David, I went to Berlin to interview the Royal Welch Fusiliers, as the Wall lay in souvenir bits around our boots. Before those stories were filed, I was on the phone to our lads in the Gulf, organising support groups for families and female penpals in every town or hamlet we covered. With my free hand, oblivious to the labours of others, I wrote recipes, wedding reports, news pages, teen pages, centre pages and women's pages. I loved the office, with its tensions, smoke, smells, sexism, bad light, misunderstandings and insults. I enjoyed its challenge and nerve-jangling stimulus: I was their first-ever 45-year-old junior reporter. For twenty-five years I had not looked for an easy time, or to be taken care of, seeking only approval, and not expecting or asking for fairness or good pay or a pension plan. Conditioned, irrevocably, it seemed, by those few bars of 'Clementine' at my father's knee, I was to spend a lifetime in an anguish of doubt and self-negation; fearing and inviting contumely; familiar only with the milky echoes of the threat of replacement; in need of redemption; to be returned to my proper place in the universe; to be lovable once more.

The doctor wears a look of faint alarm, watching me pull at a thread on my cloth handbag, tears bouncing off my knuckles.

"So I think we'll arrange for counselling, since you need more help than I can give you, Johanna."

As I've grown more weepy at each visit, she's finally observed that my problem is far from physical. I am grateful to her for bearing with me as I blub, and to the boyfriend who plays Scrabble with me, and cooks my food, while I lie gazing blankly at the carnation-pink woodchip wallpaper.

I have come to a complete halt: the bedroom wall is all I can see ahead of me.

"You're in serious straits," the young man observes, when I

won't get up for breakfast one morning.

By the time I am having weekly hypnotherapy sessions, my twenty-eight-year-old boyfriend, Al, to whom I was introduced by an office colleague a month before his college course started, has gone away to train as a teacher.

But Mary is already beginning to hint at a picture that I've long and wearily cherished, urging me to start being kinder to myself, and to generate a more creative life in my little house. Mary isn't being irresponsible - she does seem to think it feasible: she knows that somehow I'll make a living, from this and that: and she has a healthy belief that one ought to try, at least, to be happy. She suggests a behaviour modification programme - which includes saying no, nicely, when I mean it, explaining my reasons in a gently assertive way, and choosing what I want to do, instead of wondering what, for instance, the lady in the fish shop might.

One afternoon, after a trance-induced hot-air balloon-ride over some Nordic forests and lakes, while Mary sits opposite on the sofa, I talk to my two-and-a-half-year-old self in sonorous tones, telling her it's alright now, she is loved and happy: no one has meant her to feel bad, and she has not been rejected. Bored and unconvinced by this pantomime, Mary plays a relaxation tape instead, coaxing me to feel heavy-limbed, as the seagulls drift overhead.

We are now at age nineteen, and I am having a telephone conversation with the man I will marry. The hypnotised hand holding the receiver starts to sweat, as Frank complains to and about me.

"That awful, piping grammar school voice - can't you do something about it?"

"Five, four, three, two, one - you're waking up, bright and happy and relaxed - and we've got to get Frank out of your system," announces Mary, already having dismissed Al, as far as she is concerned, through a bit of transactional analysis and straight thinking.

"You've got to stop seeing men as parent figures," she insists: "Try behaving adult-to-adult."

But I am wilting under Mary's brisk questioning about my life. I am beginning to discern a pattern, a need to re-create that primal scene: to endure and resolve the shocking experience of annihilation in the back of the taxi.

In Al, I seek yet another improbable solution to my neurotic misery: nineteen years my junior, he is the perfect package: immature and capricious - and, in sinister addition, the age of Frank at our marriage.

Mary remains frozen-faced when I tell her the age gap is such a problem to him that Al can't commit himself to me, and believes he might one day want to 'go through the mill', complete with a dozen children surrounding a groaning trestle table.

"I think we're letting Al off a little too lightly here. People get over all sorts of problems if they really love each other. You're just rubbing salt in the wound."

I'm encouraged, but it's an ancient bruise, and, as soon as Mary leaves, I immediately revert to the familiar dependent state; phoning him from my lonely fireside rug while he smokes dope in his room with college girls.

My heart bleeds for myself at the tableaux I've single-handedly constructed: I've stopping seeing most of my old friends, having cunningly mapped out a gradual role-reversal so that he becomes the career person and I lie gibbering and penniless - it is a ruthlessly scripted part, where I am totally at his mercy.

The lyrics of 'Clementine' have lain enseamed in my soul for too long, and, as I pick up his ashtray or wash his shirts, my identity dissolves - no longer am I journalist, poet, parent, painter, student, English teacher or diarist.

"You've written all this stuff? All this time writing in your diary you could have been doing something productive," says Al, respectful of, but incredulous at the sixty full exercise books bursting out of an old suitcase.

"You're a writer but you're avoiding it. Next time you get the urge to spend an hour wallowing in your feelings about Al, do some proper work instead," says my friend, Phoebe.

"The diary is the art, maybe?" says my unsentimental,

pragmatic sister, Lottie, born a thousand days after I was.

My counselling sessions with Mary end, and I seem to be able to function a bit better: I buy a word processor, resign from the newspaper, and phone round the schools for some supply teaching.

Phoebe, studiously ignoring the charm of my grime and cobwebs, buys me a feather duster, and I listen to the radio, to chat shows and history and arts programmes. I wash the pots attentively, scour the taps, soak the grill pan and dry out the damp salt by the fire. It is no longer necessary for me to have my finger on the news pulse: I can absorb, ruminate and potter for a few months: the bank now owns the house and has lent me a couple of thousand pounds. But I will soon be fifty, so it is sink or swim - though I am planning to tread water for a little while, until I have found my bright water-wings: then, I tell myself, I will dog-paddle through those pathological deeps to Day One Thousand - and swim right back, *sans* the sad song of 'Clementine'.

I get my first call for school one winter evening. At dawn, I linger for a long while on the path outside my house, looking back at the thin mist of snow on the Carneddau, as the mountains come to life. Peewits and seagulls call in the silence over the Menai Straits, as I tread the road down to the station.

From my Sprinter window, I watch the energies of wave and wind and permanences of rock and sand, as the sky grows peachy and cold, and at the reflections of a girl from the bank and a fat teacher she's talking to: she knows all about bank charges and is going to the Caribbean with her boyfriend for a holiday next year: this very morning she nearly forgot to leave the garage open for the decorator to get his materials.

Blimey, what if she hadn't?

Piers stand in the ocean as I make this coastal trip on odd days during the following weeks, strings of lights blow along proms in the morning wind, quarries show their slabbed and slimy sides, caravans speck fields of mud, little empty cafés stand alone on tracts of sand and marram grass. Faces lie opposite me in the puddle of the glass door when the train stops, and I press the button to get out.

At school I am often first in, hit by the wave of warmth, and the caretaker's greeting, looking at my reflection in the panelled glass, over photos of a dance display and teenagers playing tin drums with snake-hipped West Indian actors. In the staff lavatory, I blink at myself, flatten my hair, redo my makeup, straighten my tights.

l notice a 2H pencil lying on the white counter, under the mirror.

Teachers filter into the staffroom in my wake: "I thought you were in because I recognised your coat," one or another says to me.

Easy to recognise, my coat, because it looks as if half a dozen tramps have slept in it: but I like that look. I like the organic change in that coat, since I bought it for fifty pounds in Harwich years ago.

It's easy to recognise their coats, too. They are usually new and have not been anywhere near a tramp; they prefer a habitat of umbrellas, wallets, theatre tickets and dry cleaning bills to maintain their perpetual, bright woolly nap.

(Whose is the pencil? 2H is too hard and faint for anything I might be thinking of drawing, so I leave it there.)

In the staffroom I look on the yellow list to find my work and to see what the other supply teachers are doing, and I ask if I have to mark a register, then go up to the lab or along to the music room or into the sixth form area or the Welsh mobile, sign the notes from children who've been ill, and take the register at the desk, filling in the red circles with N or L or V - a note, a late, a family vacation.

"Have we got you, Miss? Wha-oh!"

"Oh, my God, it's her."

"Where's Mr Gold? I've got homework for him. Needn't have bothered." And so on.

Then break - I take out my flask and moon around the room, looking at posters telling me how God came to Abraham, or how fiords are made.

It is calming being inside the organisation - soothing to look at busy people with important work and messages and meetings to go to; interesting, sometimes touching, to chat with the first-formers and hear their worries. I swim about in the little pond and pieces of bread in the form of half a day here or there will be thrown to me; and there will be envy among the supply teachers, of those who've received a huge loaf of three or four weeks - but it is all the same; we all have to swim round and round for the work.

I like it fine, but I like it better when I make tracks homeward, when I walk back up from the station and buy my groceries and come in and close the door and open a bottle of wine with my supper, and have it alone.

The supply work helps with the bills, and I start to sell a bit more writing, trying to shift the focus from my love life to my creative career. But it hurts, and I draw myself reluctantly to the word-processor: I still spend hours on the phone talking to Al - by now a teacher himself in faraway Bury. Happily settled into his teaching role, he is beginning to understand, he says, that I need time to write, but adds that he would like to be with me, when he has mastered the work, if I want him. He has deduced, he tells me, that I need the world to function on my terms absolutely. I fear this pronouncement is inspired by something dastardly he's perceived in me. I gnash my teeth at sudden flashbacks of childhood birthday parties, where laughing toddlers wait for jelly at my table, and where an impolite and chubby paw creeps up through the damask pleats, to snatch at the bright bowl of dolly mixtures, before they can be shared.

So what am I to do in the face of all this unfamiliar care and appreciation of my need for time to write? Chuck away the herring-boxes without topses for good?

I panic that my cover has been blown, that I will be forced at last to quit this lunatic closet wherein I have dallied so long. And yet, in the midst of this torment, there is a hint that his words might represent a fond bombardment of my position, and I feel bliss at the prospect of the placement of me, by a power figure, into a foreground, with the sense of background, not far from a thousand days into my early life - of being the apple of someone's eye. I am in my childhood home again - I hear my parents breathe their stories; a doll's house becomes visible through the Christmas dawn, and I hear silvery bells, and know the memory of my wax crayons, of colours I had scuffed across drawing paper as an infant, the awed sensation I haven't experienced for years, of being safe and loved and acceptable, of someone wanting me to realise my best self, of emotions slipping solidly back into their proper frame.

So there are moments of contentment in the middle of this disquieting shift: I am at one with myself from time to time as I warm my bottom against the winter fire and shop in the snow on Mondays, when Al has gone back. I think a lot, and hide from people, and write reams in my diary and a bit at the word-processor, anxious about how to coalesce those elements of my subjectiveness, my history and analysis, without making a pig's ear of it: reading reviews of new writers and elegies on the English novel, fearing my own audacity and not caring either.

And there are sudden moments of buddhahood and gentle epiphanies, as I come down in the mornings, to find books lying on the sofa in the frosted white morning light, and when I take a reel of black cotton and a reel of white, and with one sew an unravelled jumper sleeve, and with the other mend a hole in an eiderdown, where feathers fly out each day all over the bedroom. I look at the needled cotton reels lying on a white uncovered pillow; I prick my finger and watch the crimson blood seep into the hoary acrylic fibre... I am making connections, seeing through what I call 'writer's eyes' - which infuse one with the sensation that a skin has been removed from the eyeballs and a layer lifted from the object in view - as if one is being made aware of a palpitating essence which links itself to things close and far, as in a poem. I had an outbreak of 'writer's eyes' with the 2H pencil, as well as with the cotton reels; and perhaps while I gazed at the dancing stained-glass lights on my sister's coverlet. It had struck me first in Sicily, as I glanced at some sugared violets in a confectioner's window, and when I saw a field of gilded plum tomatoes lying in the sun near

Turin from the train. Everything in sight becomes suddenly connected and symbolic and reverberating and meaningful and inscapeful and celebratory and resonant. It is a silent prayer or a reminder of God or a reassurance of the perfection of the moment, where the past is fully realised in the promise of the future: indispensable to the creative life; and I know Mary, for one, would be delighted.

'Writer's eyes' make me feel better, as does Al's manly comprehension of my need to create. So why do I feel so at sea? I am selling articles: I have been approached by a poetry editor and a publisher wants to see my fiction. But it is as if, now I have the chance to redeem those years, when I have, at last, the opportunity to flesh out the one-dimensional sixties' Kodak girl who smiles and agrees outside every chemist's shop, I want nothing more than to forget art, to be a deputy head of department teaching English at a comprehensive in Bury, just like the people Al describes to me. It seems that what they are doing is infinitely more real; so I quiz him endlessly on where he sits and to whom he talks and what is said and what he wears and what he teaches each lesson and what he eats and who his friends are, and if he can live without me.

I am like a heathen child, with her nose pressed to the window of the English missionary hut, as the family inside sips Earl Grey and yawns for home.

I tug at the bone in my nose and mooch back off into the scrub: theirs is the Promised Land, alright; and Al is well and truly in there, with a diviner frame of reference than mine can ever be.

He tells me he loves me, this young man, and would be with me but he knows I must get on with my work, and thinks I should give it a chance, without having him as a distraction just yet.

He is being sympathetic, reasonable and thoughtful, so why do I feel so defeated and hurt?

Because a savage is never really loved by a missionary.

Because savages pinch sweets.

Because savages are murdering bastards, as far as missionaries are secretly concerned.

Because a two-and-a-half-year-old savage would try and shake a missionary baby out of its pram.

To remove it for good.

To have all the dolly mixtures for itself.

And - to see what would happen next.

GREEDY AND CURIOUS

"I hadn't known mam was so ill - she'd been coughing, as usual, and overnight she'd got worse, but dad hadn't realised how bad she was either, and had sent me to work in the morning."

Nine years after her mother died, and at the outbreak of war, my mother met and married my father: the second son of an army family; a lifeguard and a soldier. They settled in Rhos after I was born: at the time of Lottie's birth we lived in the flat with its red-and-black tiled kitchen floor, where, in autumn, shafts of sunlight filtered through the thin paper covering the long windows. In spring, clouds blew past the pale sun, its light picking out the raindrops on the glass, lying like light stars, or clues to existence, gleaming for an instant, then vanishing. Winters brought visits from my grandma, who, in her fur coat, with my sister and me at her feet, walked us to the promenade, to feed bread to the wheeling gulls, and take deep breaths of the air, which lay like a drug in the sinuses. Her long scarf dangled from the railings to fish us up from the beach, as the tide came swirling in, and, as the sea siphoned fluted notes, in crystalline and silver runnels over our Clarks sandals, I pushed my sister out of the way, to be the first to safety.

My father, who worked at the Ministry of Food, drew cartoons in the evenings, resting his paper on a large wooden board, rubbing out the pencilwork when the Indian ink had dried. My mother, who had wanted to be a journalist or historian, worked as a dinner lady, taught us to knit, and showed us, ignoring our apathy, how to cut meat for stews. From the age of seventeen, she had looked after others, rearing her young sisters, and keeping house for her police sergeant father. She had been packing pound bags of sugar, and stacking them on the shelves in a dingy shop in a back street of Bootle, when the news came.

My dad had picked up the baton swiftly, enabling her to run on, into womanhood and motherhood, without looking back. But for Frank and me, a flurry of dust blew up, and over the sun.

One Sunday in the summer of 1961, my mam and dad and Lottie and I travelled by train from Dinas to Wrexham, looking for student lodgings for me.

Down streets of terraced houses our suburban family walked, and before long I was settled nicely with a Mr and Mrs Jones near the Beast Market, after navigating our way around gangs of children playing with saucepans on their heads. I reflected on the dull aluminium shine and the vestless young bodies on the pavement: saucepans being alien objects to me at this stage, including small ones, as, in the boast of many a young bride then, I couldn't even boil an egg.

So I was now in digs, hurrying the mile to and from my college four times a day. Green and golden, Frank described me, reading Dylan Thomas in the fields behind, and I was soon persuaded to share a flat with two fellow-students, not far from the house near the steelworks where he lived, with his parents and son.

And all the days, full of drawing and banter, lying in cowslips with my new friends, sunbathing on warm gravestones in the spring, seemed like a poem, linked and symbolic; I was free as any hazel-eyed savage could hope to be - with a premonition of the end of childhood, scrawling inside a shoebox lid in a borrowed dressing-gown: 'Today I am nineteen years of age', and still cooking eggs in the kettle, despite the risk of anthrax, and still without the necessary saucepans and attendant trousseau - and, as perhaps I had intuited, soon to wed.

Emerging into the first decade of that early revolutionary period, I was unaware of its being a psychedelic or any other kind of atmospheric era: it was just another day, to most of us. And a lazy, bored grammar school kid who wandered off to art college had no philosophic burden - no Zen caperings had dusted, nor carafes of red wine spilled over my size five shoes: the only beat with which I was familiar usually preceded a retreat. Yet, in a trice, I was black-stockinged and duffled, sketchpad and Kerouac stuffed in my bucket bag, fringe bleached white, eyes ringed with kohl, bopping to 'Please, please me' at Friday student barbecues in the bluebell woods, blinking at *That Was The Week That Was* on Sundays, home again for the weekend, then bowling back on Monday mornings in a 3Om.p.h. lift in a Morris Minor. Back to life classes, clay modelling, rent-man's glove sketching of the brewery, sniffing the scent of hops in the cold air, walking back to my lodgings, with a polite Burmese boy, or a lad from the Valleys, one disabusing me of my fondness for the literal in pictorial art, the other pulling me away from Aston's furniture shop still life reproductions, to magazines called *Scope* or *Arena* or *Artist,* and books like *Ways of Seeing,* and teachers who talked about form, and conté crayon and masking tape.

Mrs Jones made me tomato sandwiches every day, and I shared a bed with a spotty girl from Blaenau Ffestiniog, who wore her knickers and suspender belt under her nightie, liked my hair in 'plates', and who sometimes walked with me to college, and bought a crisp green apple to eat with me on the way.

Slowly I discovered what drawing was really about, and I was good at it, and watched the older students painting their diploma figure compositions, believing I never would. I begged meat skewers from the butcher for my inky life drawing sessions, straddled the donkey, and was eyed by a compact man wearing a red neckerchief. In one fell swoop, I argued about the model's pose, finished with my schoolboy sweetheart, and turned to the dashing painter, fatefully revealing, *en route*, the old flaw. Romantic love revisited upon me the emotional vulnerability of a thousand days, where ego-boundaries faded into the mists of dependency, where I took me ducklings to the water, fell into the foaming brine. Snared anew in subjugation, all the overwhelming needs of the torn untimely two-and-a-half-year-old thirstily took up their positions, catapulting my glad self into psycho-emotional hock once more - and there went the song again: *Light she was, and like a fairy, and her shoes were number nine.....*

He had hit the C-spot, and I was a goner - caught my foot against a splinter, dreadful sorry, Clementine.

He showed me nothing, of course, but what I was already on course to learn, greedy and curious.

His experiences, however, were very different from mine: he described how, at eighteen, he had scrubbed jail passages on his hands and knees, over and over, and, when his mother and father had come to visit him, how she had cried at his red-raw, carbolic-soaped face: he told me how he had emptied his piss and shit with killers. When he came out of prison for the adolescent offence, he worked at an aircraft factory, impregnated his first bride-to-be, and painted at his easel, before his early shifts, in the spring woodlands of his boyhood. As we talked in pubs, and made friends with others, and shared books and walked home, I saw, mingled with his shame and anger, an uncompromising need for choice and discovery - to experiment in life, and to make of it art.

Frank and I stayed and worked at college all day, to walk the three miles home together later, over the 'Aggie', a long boggy meadow running alongside a stream, which soon became a path to Frank's history and my own enlightenment, in the sense of the knowledge I was to gain of Cézanne and Camus, pints of beer and pickled eggs at the bar. I had found in Frank, at last, I informed everyone, a person who could tell me things I didn't know already.

"Woman is the moon to man's sun."

"The shadows in the snow are blue."

I also learned that all your grant money could be lost in an evening's game of brag in the pub; a man can be married, divorcing, engaged and seeing someone else simultaneously; Cézanne farted while visitors watched him work; magenta oil paint showed through white primer; I blushed scarlet, but every other girl turned a 'cool pink'; other women had beautiful cheekbones, but I had a good bone structure 'if you could see it'; you could wrap your bike round a lamp-post with one hand while wearing sandals and a cravat, and read Auden with the other; you could sleep on bales of stolen hay in fields all night, and eat digestive biscuits and drink tea in cafés in the morning.

Frank, a hazel-eyed savage himself, showed me poems like 'Lisbie Brown' and 'The Pot of Basil', and the hatched brushmarks of grim industrial landscapes, skies and hills and tawny scrubland which I would forever after see in his way, and teach others how to see, too. He showed me how the undemonstrative love of a coarse-grained father, the anguish of a bereaved mother, tragic after the loss of her firstborn daughter, has its effect, too, on an infant artist nature, and not always Clementine.

I was twenty when we married and Seb was born: we would never again be outrageous drinking partners and critical, avaricious exhibition-goers. In the year that followed, I exacerbated his nervy snobbery: I snatched at strawberries at a Liverpool garden party, angered him with my working-class manners, my grating voice, my grammar school insouciance, my dependence on my parents, my unawakened sensibilities, my shallowness and youth, my vanity and spontaneity.

So that he would spend the evenings, after teaching his night class, in the Peppermint Lounge, or the Blue Angel, while I would try to get the baby to sleep. Seb would wake and blink in the electric light, and stand crying and perplexed at his cot bars, haloed with matted gold fuzz from his hot pillow. And, despite the tang of the city's oily river and our vivid new friends, the poetry and the painters, the spawning of a dual identity, we were no longer the fabulous pair we had once, briefly, been, but squabbling co-habitors, with winking envies and secrets, and private schemes for survival, and sad vestiges of our selves flashing in sarcasms and suspicions as I asked for money, and he roared off in his little black van.

Today, I regard in my garden the young comprehensive schoolteacher, standing with his secateurs at the ivy bush, in his black cotton shorts and a white tee-shirt decorated with an insurance firm's logo, sawing branches, and loudly swearing. The wind blows softly against my skin, as it had in Sicily, when the sea water had dried in lacy patterns.

Al has bought me a set of water-colours and, as he works, I surreptitiously unwrap the tablets of colour, and lick my little finger, stroking it over the emerald and indigo squares to moisten them, then start a picture on a piece of rag paper. First, I drag a blue for the sea, and seconds later above the waves a vermilion sun hangs, just as it used to in the paintings I did at nine or ten, when I'd discovered that heraldic scarlet in a cheap box of my own. Next, a spread of warmly glowing viridian, layering over the translucent ocean, and redder yet reflections in the sea, caught at its billow edges - five minutes after opening the box, and we are brimful of breezes and Pandora panfuls, tongues blueberry, red in tooth and fingernail.

"Brushes! You need brushes!" cries the lad, on seeing my preoccupations, and disappears into the house.

"I just don't belong to that world," I had told friends with jobs in local schools, as I wrote to an address on a torn-off piece of a newspaper someone had given me.

'That world' held an ambivalent fascination, and was the one my father respected, of pension plans and job security. I sensed that being adult meant participating in what I criticised as a dull and predictable status quo, but, while I might have needed its affirmations, I desired more to become authentic in my own instinctual way. So I took the foreign job, and, twenty years ago, trekked east, to ignore for another season the valerian bobbing pinkly from the hillsides, and my own few yards of grass, my apple trees and lilacs, my honeysuckle and purple loose-strife, my philadelphus and privet.

With the idea of taking Seb with me on the train to a home found for us by my new boss, I was all set to be a teacher of English at the 'smile' town of Augusta, as far as I could make it from the missionary life and the comprehensive schoolroom.

Then, one sunny afternoon, Frank arrived, and insisted on Seb's schooling, in Liverpool.

"OK. I'll go with Dad," said the tactful, clear-eyed boy.

So, unexpectedly alone, separated for the first time from my son, I set off to the new culture, to a muddled idea of sun and Lawrentian blood-knowledge, and away from the country which had defined me.

In a dream I lived and taught, in heat and storms and floods; sharing an umbrella with old Sicilian women in the cobbled streets; waving to students from the balcony, where swallows swirled above the evening promenaders. My boss flirted with me: "You have fallen out of the sky!" and others showed me dolphins and dinner parties. For a time I believed that the road to freedom might be in the company of the immature trades union representative, from the Esso refinery, with his copy of *L'Unità* under his arm, one eye half-closed above his cigarette and his soliloquies.

"It is the end of the Communist Party in Italy!"

"The heads of our leaders are full of shit!"

"I'll start a party of my own - a real party for the workers!"

"I will withdraw from the lists!"

I was impressed by Enzo's political awareness; his seeming integrity. He was a thinker and a revolutionary, I decided, as we drank beer after my classes. He scoffed at my hosts, at the influence of America on his fellow-countrymen, at the patriarchal traditions. I sympathised with his frustration, the conditions in which he worked. I admired his solid friendships among the refinery workers, and his attempts to better himself by learning English. His lugubrious remarks would later flatter and inspire me.

"No one has looked after you, my little wooden soldier."

"Be the furious woman more often, *principessa*!"

But it was his moodiness, his huffy not wanting to do things which flushed my soul with rapture. I would call for him at the apartment, where his father in huge blue jeans ate spaghetti, and his black-shawled mother returned heavily from market with remnants of cloth to sew. If he had dramatised a slight, or was weighed down with the world's impercipience, he would only stare and mutter, "*Non ho la voglia* - I don't want to."

We sat one evening in the Greek theatre at Syracuse in the southern light, as the sun burnished the faces and bodies of the young couples who lay with their heads in one another's lap, and the stone reflected the light and heat. Enzo was reading the introductory notes to the play aloud to me: "We all have a savage side to our nature, which we ignore at our peril." The drama seemed to emphasise my idea of relinquishing the safe parameters of Britain, and I began to believe that I might discover something about how to live, in this melodramatic society: I might find some roots and some dignity.

In today's *dalliance sur l'herbe*, my present hero saws down the ivy, and sings - growing, to my eyes, more perfect with every few bars - and then his arms begin to bulge like Bluto's through the undergrowth, his legs burst from the shorts like cut-glass goblets, his neck strains like a minotaur's from the green maze, his face is an impassive icon; his ash-blond hair gold thread, his skin abruptly brushed with celestial dew.

"You'll need some weedkiller, Johanna."

At this, bands of cherubim silver the far clouds, and the ivy yields further bounty as a bit of old electrical wire lands in my lap. Mountains pick up their snowy skirts, tiptoeing to their assigned place in the new geography; the seas part as he stalks his ineffable destiny; lepers are whole; dead men rise smiling to their keening wives.

The breeze is cooler and the sea platinum in the evening, when he leaves: a small bush of starry white blooms dapples the pile of fir branches, now nestling in a pale green maidenhair fern which has spread lightly over the years to cover several square feet at the corner of the garden. A plane vapour blows over the sun: I look up to see the clouds churning in the sky, and down at the shiny buttercups at my feet, and hear the squawk of seagulls and the cheep of sparrows, as I have for years.

And as I look, in the old solitude, over the pale strands of ocean, I am bereft.

With the water-colours, I paint a picture of the garden,

pushing colour out of the apple blossom and its leaves, too rosy and too hotly bright, and make pale Turneresque representation of the distant blue gate, rosy streak of cloud and dripping grey of evening: the garden chair looks set for take-off past the pots of geraniums, while a stripe of rusty red forms the border of hydrangea, foxglove and rose. Then I begin to add bits of umber and scarlet from the black box, dipping the wet brush into the petals to spread colourlessness and let the white of the page in through the pink; unburdening the picture further by removing more layers of colour: revealing and creating new possibilities; peeling the onion and dipping the brush.

My heart is banging in my chest, because Al has had a lift home from the Parents' Evening with Molly Pratt, the young history teacher .

"The writing's on the wall," I explode. "We might as well finish it now. I'm not spending another year like this."

It would even be a relief in a way, I think: if I don't have a choice, I will not worry; if there is no white in the box of water colours; if I'm supposed to use the paper showing through instead, I will; my world can as easily be made up of three sorts of green, two blues, two reds, a yellow and a few indeterminate browns.

Can't it?

IGNEOUS

As I hang my coat in a cubby-hole, next to the staffroom, I notice a Brenda Chamberlain picture on the wall. Do they see, I wonder, this pen and ink wash of three fish and a scrunched-up cloth, the delicately-patterned jug? The composition is strong; the drawing sensitive, tracing the ugly lips of the fat cod's head as if they are the petals of a threatened species of wildflower: the whole mix of fish, jug and tablecloth cascading impetuously across the paper. The motions of the real world seem stilled in this arresting of harmonies, but the air is mottled with hysteria at the impending government inspection, and chalky with dull chat about cars - it is as it has been in every school I've worked in since I threw away my teaching practice notes, and caught the train to Sicily.

Today I'm teaching art, I'm pleased to see on the wall list - but first, maths.

The wind is keening round the school buildings today, and the sun shines weakly over the rooftops where workmen apply pitch, and their jackets blow up over their backs in the breeze. A little girl yawns over her fractions and flow charts, protractors and pictograms, and sits back, stretching out her legs in white socks and black boots: I wonder if she is as engrossed as I once was.

"Did Jean eat more cakes than Betty?" she asks, crossly.

"Can I draw the cakes and the cups, Miss?"

"In this party you have to pay for the lemonade
and the cake."

"Not much of a party, is it?"

"No, more of a disco, Miss."

"What does this mean - 'least'?"

In the room next to mine, I hear a female teacher explaining 'igneous', 'sedimentary' and 'metamorphic' to a class in its study of rocks: I listen to the definition: 'igneous rock is produced by solidification of the earth's internal molten material'.

"So, Miss, it can't ever change?"

"That's right."

And I hear her laughing into the blue at some mistake of her own.

By the end of the afternoon, an inarticulate blond child and I are both stained in the red powder paint with which he has filled a paper plane, in the quiet of the store-room, and thrown around. The whole place, including the boy's shirtcuffs and the parquet floor, is layered in a lurid volcanic ash, which the caretaker, turnip-faced in a grey overall, his smug bucket clanking in the emptying school corridors, refuses to mop up.

"It's like someone's been painting the post office. How long did you leave him in there? "

Dismally, I brush up what I can, leaving smears of dirty red dust clinging to the old cupboards, and the splintered chevrons of light and dark wood I stand upon. I trail home in a sudden storm, sit on the bus in my wet mac, and rub the steamy window while my elbow grows damp in the guttering water along the sill.

At home, waiting by my phone in the moist, cool day, I take up a photograph of Seb at sixteen, with his thick, blond fringe. He is leaning on the garden wall, stroking our ginger cat. I remember he had been painting the window frames that afternoon, chatting to me, on the garden seat.

Al is is telling me he would very much like it if I would go to live with him, when the time is right.

"Why don't you ever say 'want'?" I ask wearily, and look old in my reflection in the glass of the photograph of my son. I notice some baby conkers have blown off the trees, and it is not even Midsummer's Day, but grey and growing late.

Seb is here for the weekend with his girlfriend, Fay. He drives us to a beach, where he wriggles into his wetsuit. She shivers, then wanders off to look at wild flowers, like the lips of dead cod in the meadows, while my son floats in the water, his blond hair spread out, studying crabs with striped colouring, and buoyant seaweeds - 'like flying over a jungle', and I watch the sun's sporadic reflection as he swims, breaking in pools like the moon in a Zen poem, inky and heavy in parts, wobbling and shining and disintegrating into fronds of pearl and silver, with the seaweed swaying in black and brown bunches in the water's heavy movement, as he plunges for shrimps and tiger crabs, and his head emerges, eyes blinking above the pink snorkel, face smeary and pale behind the goggles. As he chases creatures with a plastic bag, I am reminded of him as a small boy, when I watched him play, and the seagulls cry, and the waves hit the sharp rocks, to run charmingly and guiltlessly and cruelly along the shore.

We walk to the black rocks at the tip of the peninsula, and sit on the crags, glazed with yellow-green lichens and tufted with pink thrift. We watch a seal fishing: the sleek head rising, then plopping back. The great, green waves wash powerfully against the dark cliffs and the pebbly beach, as the sunshine just shows, through low cloud, and Seb and his girl cuddle together for warmth. Then we move inland, as a mist blows in from the sea, to where foxgloves loom and moss roses peep dewily, in the chill and stilly glades. The two melt into the distance, elementally absorbed. I watch a brook's mellow liquids spilling silkily over boulders, their velvety roundness cupped in the damp grass. In such woodland, where small white flowers show through, like a speckling of snow, we had shared our one-parent home with Lottie and her daughter Juliet.

"I feel awkward - the other women are looking at me," Lottie said, as we collected our children from the school where I worked as a dinnerlady, ploughing to and fro, in my long blue overall and cotton cap, bringing home in my canvas bag the food that should have gone to the pigs - bowls of gleaming green jelly, set as still as valley ponds, and roast spuds with glistening, crispy fat, like the water which frothed on river rocks - ignoring the sudden lining of working boots in the hallway, and the petalling of nurseryman's shirts on her bedroom floor.

"I needed to be married - I didn't like living without a man."

She described how horrified she'd been as an infant, when I moved up to the grammar school, and she was left to fend for herself.

"I had to pay my own dinner-money, and walk to the teacher's desk with the money for the savings stamp. I'd always had someone to take care of things - I'd never known life without you in charge, when we were kids, so marriage was just an extension of that."

"Are you listening to it? Radio Four? I have it on all day while I'm working. AIDS. CJD. Old age. They scare you to death with that, and the next thing you know it's *Moneybox* - they're advising you about pension schemes so you can go windsurfing - but there won't be any bloody retirement for you, don't you forget it - if you're still with us, all you'll be doing by then is sitting round in the old folk's home, with the wrong drops for your eyes, and no one on the staff listening to anything you tell them.... I'm a vegetarian now. I live on pulses and chickpeas and grow my own courgettes in the backyard. Did you see the thing in the paper about the age of the food we're eating? Fish nine years old? 'Fresh from the pod' peas that have been frozen for months? We think our parents were brainwashed hicks, coming to the cities to work - but they still made sure they got a piece of homekilled beef and a good cauliflower. I watch these women from the banks in their black suits parking their Fiestas in my street and darting off to the supermarket for giraffe tikka or whatever they buy, and they're told on the packet what wine to drink with it..... even taste is dictated to us, and it's all a bloody con."

Fred's junk shop window looks out onto a street of net-curtained terraced houses.

"The big industrialists are in charge of it all, I reckon. They control the entertainment, the food, the art...and I'm worried about those Michelangelos that have been ballsed up while they're being cleaned. Irrevocably damaged, I bet, and there goes a bit more culture. No one cares. It's all a con. Even my cat is a con-man. We're all supposed to be fooled by this anthropomorphic crap - like the Serengeti cheetah, did you see that programme? - 'How beautifully they move', and so on, but really they're just predators, too. I say to my cat, 'You just eat and sleep and shit, don't you?' Everyone's on the make. This country is sick."

To Fred, even producing art is impossible, because true artists - revolutionary, visionary, iconoclastic - are, of necessity, outsiders. Our present society doesn't, he insists, want anything of art, despite the lip-service and homage paid to it; artists have ultimately to be made to fit; so he has become a forger.

"And have you noticed the journalism? Those art reviews - it's all so right-wing, even in the leftish papers. All we get is Wagner and *The Ring* and bloody Benjamin Britten ...the sort of stuff we oiks - and that's what we are to them - can't afford to go and hear, but which is all grant-aided, for them. And Foucault! Bloody brilliant ideas, so they're out to get him, aren't they? So all they talk about is his homosexuality. They criticise him on one arts programme, and then a repeat the following week - never done that before, I notice...get the boot in good and proper...totally demolished him - and this is supposed to be a culture that encourages art."

In his forgeries, Fred is secretly developing a glaze similar to that used by the old masters, and he uses it in his paintings of sailing ships, or on the 'antique' wooden chests with lids where Jessica the Ewe or Basil the Bull baa and bellow their way to shopping malls in New York and Adelaide.

"They say they've got special equipment to analyse that glaze and it can't be recreated - that there are blobs of candle wax and soot in the paint. Bollocks."

Privately he works on portraits of women he has known, from photographs or memory, with fine layers of translucent washes shaping cheek or the white of an eye, oblique glances, tangles of hair, dissolving into background until the sense is of the dematerialisation of any personality: and it seems that femaleness, in and of itself, has become a terrifying, cardinal force in the painter's life. He can't remember much about the marriage, he says now, which begat four children, or his life in the big house on the estuary.

"To think I was head of a department! That I was at the Slade! That I used to row and play cricket for the county! "

He calls me to complain about his dealer, Ronnie, or to talk about painting or love, or to hint at the thing that has spoiled his relationships with women all his life.

This week, heavy rains have brought floods, and he takes me to the back of the shop. The wet carpet is piled high with tools and bric-à-brac. Fred is in the process of cutting out squares of the damaged needlecord, removing each loaded piece, throwing away what he thinks he doesn't need from the selection of stuff in front of him, then keeping the rest, so that a higgledy-piggledy pile of usable spanners and nails is now growing in the room.

"I'm an outsider - you know Camus' *Outsider* ? - it's me."

The liquid brown eyes are full of emotion, as he talks about his sense of alienation, his lifelong inability to take control.

"What really hurts me now is when I'm with the kids - there are things I could help them with. But there's all that time gone, and I just wasn't in their lives, and there's nothing to be done about it. It's sad, and I don't know what happened."

So he paints the fat pink pigs on chests which will be shipped abroad, develops his ideas about colour, hangs round at the edges of the established provincial art coteries in his Oxfam jackets and trousers, smokes his roll-ups, observes the pool players in his local, grows pots of basil and parsley.

Among his old lathes and bikes and engraving equipment, railing still against the status quo, he talks about his latest woman friend.

"No, it's nothing - completely out of the question. It's just that she's so different from anyone else in my life. It's fascinating. These people, like her, they fit you into their diary when they're at a loose end. She rings me up when she's bored, and I admit it, I'm lonely. But there's more there than meets the eye - there's a novel, now, if you want one."

Fred owned this place when we met years ago and I wanted somewhere to write.

"Yes, OK," he said, over his shoulder, in the pub, so I took my boxes of books and set up in the spare room.

In a downstairs back space, when I lived there, he'd built a pottery and kiln, and, when no one was buying books or clothes or records, he'd fire his pots, with the sparks flying out through the cracks in the chimney over him, while I wrote my stories in my little room, warmed by a paraffin heater on the bare boards, and looked through the grimy window at the slate tips in the rain, and thought of Jack Kerouac.

"Listen, if you want to write a novel, listen to this one...."

Mellow songs by Joan Armatrading from the record-player by the till lingered in the air, and he admired a complexion or deciphered a psychology, *sotto voce,* to me, and together we quoted from Karen Horney's *Inner Conflicts.* He told me of his breakdown after his divorce, of daily life in the mental hospital, where it 'took all fucking day to get a cup of tea to your lips' and of drinking bouts with beautiful alcoholics, in allusive, cryptic, self-parodying anecdotes.

"I don't know what she was doing with me anyway - probably researching for her Ph.D. One of these days, I'll find my life and times in one of these psychology books someone's thrown out."

But women who were drawn to Fred never forgot him: this honest, original personality of genius, obsessed by beauty, always in the wrong clothes, whose pictures are rejected by galleries because of woodworm in the frame, a man flawed by a terrifying defensiveness and self-effacement.

In seafront towns on autumn nights, Fred and I looked up into the sky at the stars, through misty clouds which flew past in the wind. Once, the seagulls, lit from underneath, from the lights of the streets and the prom, seemed like fat stars themselves, falling in clusters, gathering in the heavens, then dropping suddenly towards the earth, luminous, and starry-white: the shapes were of stars, and they fell in groups like showers of stars, and were silent in the wispy trails.

We talked about art, and I watched the skies change colour in wintry sunsets, as I had at eighteen, with Frank. In many ways, Fred resembled him: the two were the same age; two sides of the same coin - both artists, who at some early point had made a dull, subconscious flail for survival, and were now fetched up on opposite shores: Frank of the world; Fred merely in it.

"I've never been able to get involved with any of it. I'm not in control of my life, yet I think that not taking control of your life is a crime," he would say, rolling a cigarette, after chopping onions and preparing our evening meal in the upstairs kitchen. To the cat he would remark that dependency turned one into a coward; that an artist had to be a person of courage; and as he once rummaged through a box of books that someone had brought in, he handed me a copy of *Siddhartha*.

"Here. Read that if you want to find a way of looking at life."

"What's it about?"

"It's the story of a quest for enlightenment. It's about finding and losing the self."

In my room at Fred's shop, I read how alone Siddhartha felt, when, in his search for peace, he became aware of his selfhood. He was connected no longer to his family, or to the monk his friend Govinda had become, or to the fraternity of monks, or even to the lowliest band of hermits. He asked himself whose life would he share; whose language would he speak; where did he belong? Overwhelmed by a bitter despair, he 'stood alone like a star in the heavens'. I read and re-read, until the pain of his awakening when Siddhartha walked 'quickly and impatiently no longer homewards, no longer to his father, no longer looking backwards.'

Seb had a place at a local art college, and was excited with the course, drawing pictures at night through his bedroom window. I decided to go and teach English again - I stuck a pin in a map of Greece.

"Go on, then you little devil, you," Fred said, waving me off.

And away I went, to another place; away, away - not to mimosa-filled breezes this time, but to the smell of petrol fumes, and the furore of a brittle, jangling civilisation, overlaying the blunt simplicities of temple ruins, and the pebbles of the Parthenon. I waited for my new companions on the quay, for the ferry to the islands, after a Saturday morning class, where children chanted declensions, mimicking my accent, laughing at me, as, in the evening at home, they did at Benny Hill.

On the plane, as I had looked down over the arid countryside, I remembered Horace: 'They change their sky, not their mind, who scour across the sea.'

Yet still I was to continue in my folly: bustling through stations like Omonia, strewn with blind beggars, and the flux of students; Americans, Japanese, German and Dutch, as well as my own countrymen. The days and months seemed merely stamped to silver leaf, reflecting only the same swing of sky that had hung across the nettles and ladybirds of infancy, without parameter or daytime star, as the silent seconds thrummed away. The train swayed back to Piraeus from Athens, and I stood, with a wilting spider plant for my flat, while at home my own geraniums stood desiccated on the sill, and the watering can stayed dry.

Fred hands me a book from the debris: *Experimental Lives*.

"That's you," I thought, he says, opening it at a chapter on George Sand, called 'The Free Woman'.

"What's he up to, then? Does he want to marry you, or doesn't he?" he asks half-heartedly of Al, and I see how Fred's real, unacknowledged concern has always been with his own Day One Thousand, that all these years he's been at its mercy, and, at fifty-eight, as he weeds out good tool from bad on the wet floor, he knows he is a painter, and is just beginning to understand the fatal compulsion behind his broken marriage, to properly grieve over it, and he feels like Camus' *Outsider*. Fixed in the fired-rock shape of the romantic eccentric, he stares with stark child's eyes at symbolic lovers from behind the glass, thumb in mouth. Painter and poet, he seeks correspondences, creates makeshift habitats, hears the echoes of the subtly-sharp parental reprimand, and intuits too much from a trivial incident or an idle remark.

I find a slip of paper tucked underneath a box lid: it is a quote from Correggio: *Anch'io son pittore* - 'I, too, am a painter.'

And underneath:

'Six free-range eggs
Half an ounce of Old Holborn
Garlic
Root ginger
Anchor butter'.

LOST GOLD

In memory of my son, while he is young
And of my self, now I am old
And of my husband
And our lost gold.

A cobweb forms under a shelf: I look outside, and the isle of Anglesey is black, with a silver streak of seawater running by, on this summer night.

Frank took my left hand, to place on his mother's tablecloth, among the plates of fairy cakes and bread and butter. We had arrived from our registry office wedding in Derbyshire, where I had been earlier despatched.

For a second, she brooded on the evidence, then related the fact of the ring to her husband. Frank's dad was sunk in an armchair alongside the table in view of the television: he turned to grunt embarrassed awareness.

The stolen afternoons had gone when, as students, Frank and I roamed the fields and local rhododendron woods: losing ourselves in dark groves, where great smatterings of plum-coloured blossom spread like broken eggs across the dark-green face of the forest, erupting under and over the shrubby branches, some in bullet buds, some with half-exposed petals like petticoats: huge crowns of blooms like jungle birds. Deeper and deeper we would delve: once, we emerged from a bluebell grove, after hours of collecting the perfumed clouds of misty blue flowers hanging above the slime of the pale, etiolated stems, which lay like clumps of overcooked spaghetti on our damp chests and scratched arms. In my flat, I crammed them into milk bottles, where for weeks they stood in their frail and rotting heaps.

I followed Frank faithfully, to rivers, farms and beaches - at once woman, friend and creative equal. At home in the holidays, I'd take Lottie with me to quaysides, and draw the boats, smudging wet ink with my little finger to blur the line of sail or mast. Back at college, I stayed late, to model female figures in clay, in the dry heat of the pottery, where containers of different glazes lined the shelves, and bins were marked 'slip', and the wheel waited, smeared and dried with a fine grey film.

And I was never so free, despite his cavils. The dry-smelling room; the dusty clay, the plastic sheets and techniques I was learning for caring for my work were the affirming elements of my student life, and I lapped them up as much as the curmudgeonly advice, the capricious passion and the ambivalent loyalty Frank offered.

"Yes, yes. You've got the feeling of space. But the arms are too long. Change it. You haven't looked."

On spring evenings, I'd go up to the house on the bus, from my lodgings, to talk to him in the little room his mother had set apart. On the walls were gummed old prints of Cézanne and Van Gogh, newspaper cuttings of Brigitte Bardot in French nightclubs, Sunday supplement fashion shots. Here, serious and intent, I would make collages of Bostik and paper, and his mother would knock at the door and bring in the supper of cheese and tomatoes that I never ate, from awe and nervousness and infatuation.

I'd been offered a fine art course at a college near Frank's in Reading: I was pregnant.

"You can do it - you can have the baby and still do your work."

But I had given up the course, choosing instead to be his wife, and now sitting stiffly as a stranger, in this front parlour world of uncles and cousins.

"Do you want dinner?" his mother asked me, every day,

taking her own meals alone, before or after the men, moving sadly through the steam from the sprouts and the sixteen shirts to be washed and ironed, in a house leaden with male presence - except for the back parlour, a shrine to the daughter who had died of rheumatic fever. This room was solid and reassuring in its way, but even on sunny days there was a morbidity in its corners and cloths. I knew that hearts here were as heavy and immovable as the mahogany dressers and sideboards which seemed to sigh in grief. There never seemed a summer there: in subsequent years, the wintry love had frozen in pools of duty, resentment and unexplored despair. They waited, like babes in the wood, for someone to tell them why a daughter had to die.

On Christmas Eve, while Frank went out with our old friends, I washed the lino with my mother-in-law, cheered on by Bugs Bunny. A year earlier, in the same pubs, from the lavatory at closing time, I had heard him arguing in my defence to an older, sceptical friend.

"She's alright. She's good. She's very aware."

His mother knitted me a balaclava, when Frank was at the betting shop or the races, or listening with our painter and erstwhile student friends to Wilde's *Salome* on the pub radio, and I talked to no one of the *Alexandria Quartet,* or the shadows in the snow. Friends who came back to drop him off would say, "If you two can't make it, who can?"

Frank's ex-wife came to visit her small son, who lived here too, and I would sit, technically on honeymoon, excluded once again, on what had been their marital bed, shivering and pregnant and waiting for her to go. Through the window, I drew the grey-green, wilting cabbages on the allotment, planted on a hill where the washing blew, which ran up to the railway line to the steelworks. Here I lived with Frank, married again, a father-to-be again, and not even doing proper work, in his dad's eyes.

Sam was a Geordie, an eater of pigs' trotters, and a building site foreman. But he was unfamiliar with, and reluctant to be associated with, the bohemianism and suspect morality of his artist son. Bereaved of a daughter, his first-born, how could he be reconciled to these habits of listening to poets on the radio, or this practice of taking easels and paintboxes to fields and woods?

Our relationship was polite and oblique, since I, too, belonged to that world.

"I'm tired of lying in this mudpack," he would say, on behalf of the baby, crying in his pram, on later visits. And as I could take his criticisms to heart, and secretly collude in his judgements, so I could condone the patriarch in his son, and could metamorphose seamlessly into the milk-spotted wife among the laundry, at liquid ease with his paternalism and summary condemning of all things 'fancy': readily succumbing to what I translated as mastery.

A sheaf of susceptibilities, I relinquished all sense of myself as good or talented, and the extraordinary freedoms which might fly from that, content instead to smart, to glance, wounded, from under my woollen hood, as father and son made me invisible in the cabbage stems.

With the baby due any day, and my husband trapped and indignant, in a skein of lost liberty, we came to leave, to travel south for his teacher training course: husband and wife, with two bowls for our porridge, and two spoons to eat it with.

"You grade the colours - all the oranges, deeper and deeper, and then the yellows and so on."

He would leave me with colour charts to complete, to keep me amused in the bedsit, while he was at his lectures, and I would try to hang out his shirts as his mother had.

At the beginning of the new year, we were living in a tiny attic flat, when I went into labour, as Frank stirred porridge over the black paraffin stove.

"I have a son! I am a mother!" I beamed, in Battle Hospital, falling in love with time itself, as I watched the soft January snow fall against the window, snug in the warm ward. Frank came to visit me.

"Tell them we've got a home help."

So I returned early to the two rooms, where a Baby Belling cooker, operated by shilling pieces, stood glumly on the landing between. Downstairs was the hot water, in the bathroom we shared with a Muslim family. The nappies dried, fastened to our sloping attic roof with drawing pins, Frank made plastic pants from blue laundry bags, and I found the draft of a letter to a girl: "Sorry. The mixture as before."

Thence, since the place was hopeless, to a chalet in Orwell's Binfield, where Frank prepared his teaching practice notes, and I learned to better breastfeed the baby, and heard myself say, "Put the bottles out, will you?"

In the evenings, as I awaited my husband's return on his scooter, the nappies hung bluely on the line. I sat reading on the step, while Seb crooned happily at his own hands in the air. I dyed a sheet to make myself a dress, using the window as a full-length mirror, and saw a thin, frayed face gazing back. The shadows in the snow had chilled and stilled my heart: their blueness had become the blue of oblivion.

"Why don't you do some painting? Van Gogh suffered. Think of the Chinese."

He found a job in Liverpool. The time had arrived, I believed: we would buy furniture, and have friends to dinner, and establish ourselves as a couple at last.

Our first flat was old and rat-infested, but we took Seb in his pram for walks in a little wood at the edge of the Mersey, or to the park, where Frank threw him in the air, and balloons got stuck in trees. Frank painted experimental pictures, influenced by Rauschenberg and Johns, and I would send toy trains hurtling across the floor for Seb's delight, and scamper like the rodents over the bare floorboards, or bundle the baby in his fat little quilted coat and walk him in his pushchair to the Pier Head, paying twopence for the ferry ride to Birkenhead, and cook tea on our return. I painted a picture of coloured squares, like Paul Klee, and tied it to the cot bars with bits of string. I lay in bed, with Seb in his cot, until the scuttling of the rats in the moulding, and their pointed faces winking at me was too frightening, and I picked the baby up and put him in our bed, in the big living-cum-bedroom, until Frank arrived, from teaching and nightclubbing, and we all snuggled down to sleep.

He taught all day and most evenings, so my days were spent in solitary parenting and lone, undisciplined study of English Literature: I read and answered questions on Jane Austen, and Auden, and *Hamlet*, on an Olivetti typewriter. I sat an *A*-level exam, with a roomful of sixth-formers, in a grammar school hall in the summer, in a leafy part of the city, described the Danish prince as an existentialist, and wrote a lullaby of my own, after Auden, on the spare paper. Back home, I sent frustrated letters to Lottie about my married life and my poverty, in the sixties' Liverpool, where, in ignorance of time or maturity, I warmed beef curry from a tin, or flirted with a Beatle brother, or the singer with a band, and got a little worldly attention to sustain me through the crisp, fume-filled days of shopping and fetching paraffin, and I responded gladly enough to the city streets and the autumn pavements of its outskirts.

"I smelled the leaves in the dusk, on my way back from the nursery tonight, and it just reminded me of going to night class in Wrexham."

I had indeed sniffed deep the air of my studenthood, as I pushed the pram back, under the streetlights, and believed I was forever bonded to Frank.

We moved to a Georgian terrace, near the old cathedral, where kids hung on the backs of cars, and American tourists came in search of the 'hub of the universe' that Allen Ginsberg had described. Occasionally, we'd find a baby-sitter and have a night out in the pub, and Frank met Bob Dylan there once, and I started to sell my poetry, while he painted big Pop Art pictures, or made a Union Jack from the old station clock that hung there, in accordance with the Carnaby Street mood of that swinging time, and my writer's eyes were pricked into startled, acquiescent vision.

"Heartless bitch!" Al snorts, at my table of eggs and toast and marmalade, when I tell him a story from *Experimental Lives*, where, according to Alfred de Musset, after a *nuit d'amour*, George Sand would get up to scribble her stuff. Then I sit in weariness in my garden, as he reads *The Nightrunners of Bengal,* or I lie, fifty years old, glancing up at the mackerel sky, and the newspapers smell of scorching, and a horsefly settles on my leg. I make furtive notes in a four-by-five-inch jotter, and torment him with questions about our future, in this little kitchen, whose wall is covered with photographs, and where the sun shines through the corrugated plastic roof, which I hadn't even dreamed of in those Liverpool parks.

So it seems to have its own machine, whatever we do or say, or let go or hold on to, and whichever lines of whichever songs we take to heart and our souls fester over: and whatever age we are or however profound or complex or simple our desires. Yet we cannot always be happy with the breakfast, as we ought to be, and it is still a new experience to sit alone under the apple tree for yet another summer, and it is always the same anguish - when Frank had lied to me about the Peppermint Lounge, or Al at the Pink Parrot twenty-five years on, whether I look up at ceilings of plaster moulding and pelmets where river rats peek, or at the sea changing colour from my cottage garden, where the cat licks its fur and I hear the wind blow in the wood, and the sun comes in and out all summer long, and church bells ring on Sunday mornings.

Daisies pop, inevitably, through the dew - the daisies of 'You're unreasonable because you think I should be the man about the house, and I'm not here often enough for that,' and 'You're unreasonable because you think I should spend more money on you and give you more things,' and 'You're unreasonable because you think I'm not interested in your writing and I do care and I'm very proud to see you sitting there writing in your jotter while I get the breakfast.'

After his train pulls out, I wander back in my usual Wordsworthian way, past fagged valerian and dense clouds of late elderblossom, weighing fragilely on their boughs, and the river spawning heavy dreams over the boulders, on its way seaward. I've walked this path many times, since that first October Sunday, when Al left for college, a gauche hobo, stooped and eagerly academic in his glasses, a kettle tied to his haversack. I have strolled alone along the seashore in the chill autumn wind, picking up fir cones, and been at home for the phone calls, complaining about the size of his bedsit in a seamy quarter of the city: I've heard details of endless pie-and-chip suppers, and the volume of work, and listened as the calls gradually changed into confident anecdotes about his lecturers, the new friends he made, the dope they smoked, the larks they had.

While I stammered my sadness to Mary by day, by night he recounted the tottering through Toxteth in the small hours, after conversations about love and post-structuralism. I heard of gigs in Birkenhead, where girls admired his thighs in his provincial pants, of surrealistic encounters with Scouse lasses who mocked his newly-emergent sideburns: "Laike ya saidies!" and I popped the pills, to stop the pain again.

But it is all becoming too familiar, traipsing back from the station alone after the soup and the quick packing of bags. At first, I came back and sat in the early summer sunlight, with panic in my heart and mouth. Now it is a mechanical act of putting the key in the lock, and talking to the cat as if he were human and I a true spinster: I make a tray of tea with my big mug, sort out the clothes for tomorrow's teaching, lie on the bed, look at the horse-chestnut and the shapes of its branches in the wood which I know so well, notice a leaf falling.

But why not rejoice, lick my lips, laugh at the white horses out at sea, roll over in the daisies, sing and whistle with my young lover from my own confidence and angelhood, greedy and curious for it all: be thrilled and not threatened by the essence of everyone: be glad as glad, Whitmanesque, sing in my soul and my soul's golden chains for my chance of love: see as sacred the difference between us and delightful the hope for us: swing up the babe from his Liverpool cot and bounce him towards the Liverpool skies?

I pick up socks and ash-trays, having already in anticipation lined the empty evening ahead with the papers, and the programmes I will watch, and something nice to eat or drink, as my mother advises from her own lonely widowed vantage point. She walks pensively through a glen, recalling how we picked celandines there, when my sister and I were small, and how only last week her friend and she were planning to bring picnics, and sit with a flask of tea in the sunny days ahead. But on Saturday, that friend, June, fell 'like a leaf' according to a neighbour, as she shared pea-sticks with her in her garden, and now she is alone again, with failing eyesight. I am always busy seeing Al, and Lottie is with a man called Charles, and what has been the point of it all? After all those years of doing without, and buggering up her eyes peering down the microscope at the diamond stylus factory.

"I wish Leo were alive."

The same needy girl, finding blood in her knickers at puberty, thinking she was dying: "Luckily, they were bloomers," and running home blindly at the news of her mother's death. She sighs, in her pretty navy-blue jacket with its white collar, and looks down at her white leather loafers, and thinks how she loves the greenness of this place; how gentle it is on her sore eyes. She walks along the dappled paths where we played, and made nests and harbours, and she remembers picking blackberries for 'end-of-the-month-pie', and wheeling us both in the big, black pram: Lottie peering forth in trusting astonishment, with her hair stuck out like electric wires, and me lying heavily and disgruntledly on the little sister, sucking an ice-cream, scowling at the world, resentful that once good, true and beautifully greedy and curious, I had become so discredited by the grownups.

The sun shines on my back, through my wool cardigan, as I hurry through the streets of the town. I note the chiffon floor-length dresses with white legs and heavy sandals tramping past Boots and W.H.Smith: tame girls, uneasy in nonchalant tie-at-the-waist knots, and me, captive too, schoolmarmy and be-bunned, frowning at kids in class who scrape their chairs.

Around noon, I open the sandwich box Al has tenderly prepared, and find sliced cheese and tomatoes on bread, snuggling up to a melting piece of Bury supermarket chocolate. I eat the food in a cool and shady classroom, where sweet wrappers lie on the floor, and dusty cupboards hang open.

The old part of the school, once a friary, is built of sandstone, with stained glass windows, surrounded in thick ivy. On the first floor, leading to a wide, gracious staircase, lies an arrangement of worn tombstones, with carved details of the monks who had once lived there.

As I read the note above this display, a little girl, with eyes like lead shot, asks me how many wild flowers I know, showing me her list of 'daisy, daffodil' etc. I tell her to add bluebell, moss rose and herb robert, and we talk in filtered sunshine, speckling blue and green and gold, over the tiled floor, like a palimpsest over the past, whose message is already a blur. There seems no reality to things; it is a counterfeit universe, with its sweet wrappers and wild flowers and friars' headstones, sprinkled over with stained glass lights; I stretch the thin fabric of my emotions across the stone, and see and feel through it, with eyes and fingers and an intuition of its insubstantiality.

There is only experiencing, and the reaction to that, be it Clementine or bats in the belfry or rats in the pelmet; the ferry across the Mersey or the sky over the Menai Straits; the loneliness and the new directions and old dead-ends, forever greening over and breaking off, and floating across one's field of vision.

I cast my mind over the lyrical exchange of the morning as I rose: they should make a musical of this, I think.

She: I don't want to go on like this in September - agonising about your life that I know nothing of.

He: Me neither.

She: It's mutually exploitative to carry on in a relationship without intending to deepen the commitment.

He: I agree.

She: So if you don't talk about it again or really don't seem to want to do something about it, we'll finish.

He: I'd thought that, too.

But it's not a musical.

TEA AND SYMPHONY

' ....to recognise causes, it seemed to him, is to think, and through thought alone feelings become knowledge, and are not lost, but become real and begin to mature... '

Siddhartha (Hermann Hesse)

"Am I a greenhorn? Am I callow?"

Financially insecure, yet finely caparisoned, in poetic refrains, blue eyes, witty asides, and tallness, Al skillfully assumed the role of young lover, and was soon as familiar as the kettle in my kitchen. On summer mornings, as I took the bus to the office, I would count myself blessed, leaving him with, and returning to, the breakfast dishes and Wimbledon. He brought me and quoted from his father's copy of *The Rubáiyát of Omar Khayyám*. He showed me his collection of Roman coins, and asked if I liked Sibelius. We played marbles on the carpet, and rolled small windfall apples in a game of bowls on the lawn. In the weeks I first knew him, before he left for college, I made pies and custard, and he sat next to me in the pub, in the short-sleeved shirt his mother had ironed, raising his arm protectively and awkwardly to my back, at any sign of dissension amongst the quarrelsome locals.

In general, his family disapproved of me, but the fact that his lecturer father considered me original and independent added to my charm in Al's eyes: the parent and I would exchange esoteric titbits, via the lad, and all three would be content.

"Tell your Dad: 'tea and symphony' - he'll get it," I instructed, when presenting Al with a china teapot and a classical music cassette for his birthday.

For his Friday evening arrivals, now he is teaching, I make casseroles, or lasagne and salad, or recipes he's practised with me himself. He brings wine, and steps over my threshold, blue-eyed and bleary from the school week and the train journey.

We lie in bed and I look into these myopic pools, trying to identify what quality exists there. I see the expression of a man of thirty who says he loves me. At opportune moments he says, "Pass my shirt, would you?" or switches on the televised sport, and when I ask some vital question, he doesn't hear, because of the game. Late in the afternoon, he eats the rest of last night's dinner, while I wash the dishes, vacuum the floor, make the bed, and write my thousand words for the day, and no lawns are mown, edges strimmed, or ornaments dusted.

"You don't want to be with a woman of seventy, when you're fifty, and I wouldn't want it for you," I say, from the sheets, at dawn.

"I don't want to think about it."

"We're going to have to re-jig; see what we're going to do."

"I know."

"You want me to be in the background, while you get on with your life, and I want you to be my anchor, so I'm free to write. It's impossible, because we both want a different thing."

"It's not true," says he. "I am your anchor, and I always will be."

This I need to hear, and it warms my heart still. Can it be true? Can I trust him? Will he really cook, and polish the brasses, while I sit sucking my pencil under the apple tree?

I regard his beleaguered smile; his fragilely bleak expression as he follows *Tom and Jerry*. But though I melt at the sight of his grubby-lensed spectacles, it occurs to me again how disproportionately increased in my mind is my belief in his sterling altruism and great worth: I need him to be nobler and gentler than

I am, and I make him divine, so I can cringe and become abject. When I glimpse him as ordinary it is too terrifying - I cannot bear to be bound to a normal human being who knows no more than I do, who cannot be responsible for me, but must ultimately leave me to my own devices; whose shirt sleeve I can cling onto until the end of the world, but who will never be able to save me from my own life.

He takes to his markbooks: he busies himself with rubbers and red pens.

"I'm a fool, and this relationship is inappropriate, and I'm too old for you, Al."

"Give me some help with this and stop worrying for a bit," and he takes my hand, as he looks into his registers.

"Who's Frances?"

"Who?"

"There's a message here, on this book."

He leans closer to read a scribbled note, and blushes.

"Oh, nothing. Frances Hodge. She threw a sock at me at the sports. I'd put glue in her shoes. She was the marshal. I was doing crowd control. Boring. Next year I'll be a marshal, I think."

"Next year? So you'll be there next year?"

"I mean if I'm there."

He is applying for a job nearer to me: I have seen the shirt he'll wear to the interview.

"What's Frances like? How old is she?"

But, as I begin to agonise over the details of the maths teacher's eyes, ears, nose and throat, I suddenly dry up, while he gingerly stacks his exercise books.

"I'm fed up with this. What am I wasting my time on her for? I've got more important things to think about."

"What things?"

"Er - creative things."

I fly upstairs, to sit on the bed, and I regard the recent, angry water-colour, pinned on the wall, with its plume of smoky umber, representing the silky, scented conifer we'd pruned together. His muttered responses fade in my head, as I scrutinise the picture of the tree, which now seems to be tinged with melancholic blues at its tips. Fronting the lyrical passage of curly-ironed garden seat, I see anew my gay tub of geraniums, bright swathes of lawn, and amid the blossom, a tiny green-washed apple, pendent and suggestive of an Eden to be had, in this world of delusion and delirium. From the hot red-painted border, the path fades to the blue gate. The dull evening sky, with its shimmering Rothko hint of sensuous peach, vibrates softly through distant horse-chestnut leaves, where conkers quietly burgeon. It is redolent of desirelessness, Nirvana, the Void....

On the floor, I notice a letter I've written, about his being my anchor and enabler. He has failed to pick up on my desperate articulated-in-fountain-pen needs; they have slipped off the bed and into the waters of Lethe.

He comes up to see what I'm doing.

"Let's go and get some chicken for a curry."

The butcher's lips, wet with drops of spit, are shining whitely, like his coat. With gusto, he takes the bones from the bird, telling us about his kits for making whisky, beer and gin, peach brandy and wine. He removes the pressure gauge from the top of a white plastic barrel, running his finger confidently under the lid. Blood lies under his nails and in thready channels around them, as he informs us wetly about the gas bottle. His wife, broad-hipped and blue-eyed, moves complacently to the music of the pork spheres, tidying up lumps of liver, blackened in the heat on their silver trays, sprinkled with drying flakes of herb. Back in the street, Al hesitates.

"I need one of my dad's books, from my stuff at home."

"I'll come with you."

We walk to the house from which his family has now moved: he will be joining them for a week soon, in Harrogate.

While Al rummages in his room for the book he needs, he passes me his own short stories, and I secretly read a recent letter from an ex-girlfriend, who is getting married, but will never forget what a gem Al is - so gentle, and so adoring.

He dives into a cardboard box behind a stained armchair

piled with blankets, a peaked cap atop, to show me his running medals and photos of himself playing rugby, and the sun floats on, halfway through a brindled cloud.

I think of the butcher and his wife, enviously, and I sense the window and the world outside, as our voices echo in the empty building.

The young god bestows books: Marcus Aurelius' *Stoicism*, a gift from his philosopher father, which exhorts good actions and no resentment; William Golding's *Free Fall*, resonant with self-questioning wanderings-about on a lawn. I start to talk about the books Fred and I used to read and be influenced by, before I went to Greece.

"I'd like to do something like that."

He listens to my tales of Sicily: how I'd travelled for two days and nights by train, to live with strangers.

"I could do that. But I'd go to Malaysia."

"Last night you were talking about wanting to be with me! Now you're going to Malaysia!" I screech.

Stay still sometimes under the cloud, where the sun is seen to be rolling towards the edge, and out into the blue; feel dull, mute, unable to continue, without a frame of reference or a guiding star. Fail to discern the *ignis fatuus*, be sensible only of your own smallness, and fear for your soul; only guess at what you ought to have been and done, but here begin responsibility for it; be tender to those who reach to you, and have no right to the hand you offer; know how to shroud your days in moral anguish; but learn too how to shrug it off when the spring nights come - it is worth the wait for the blue afternoons, the cobwebs veiling in the white breeze, the mazed rain and the spicy orange petals of the days ahead.

"It's here!" he cries.

'It', is a bursary I've been awarded, which will enable me to stay at home and write.

He climbs into the bed, as I open the official letter and pull out the cheque.

Beaming with satisfaction, his bony knees banging against me in insolence and missionary zeal of wit, he announces, "It'll bounce, you know."

And despite Al's sharp patella and my grief for lost youth, I am startled into anticipation, by, a promise of scope, growth and adventure, as in those times when the sun comes out unexpectedly and suddenly it's warmer; everything is colourful and more balmy. Light plays over the flowertops; the sea brightens: there are contrasts in the dapplings, and a sense of enthusiastic movement and joyful change. In moments like this we feel we have a choice: the universe seems loving and supportive.

I dress, and go to pick up the washing from the garden where it has blown off the line, with serenity blooming in me like an embryo. Peg in mouth, I stand back and admire the chiaroscuro of my existence: spades of convolvulus hearten the walls: a teatowel bellies in its small, proud way over the mad grass.

I started my book one morning, when Al was here: bringing notepad and pen to bed, and writing the first lines, despite him, and despite the emotional paralysis. In an envelope in the house lie the newspaper cuttings, poems and extracts from other novels I've begun - now I can fish about in earnest for my theme.

Schools are promptly notified of my imminent unavailability: friends and family applaud and encourage, and I tell Al that I will need total peace and quiet.

"Writers can still have relationships," he insists.

He's right, of course, I panic - look at D.H.Lawrence, 'making art of the life'.

I don't make art, though: I merely lift the latch on a lower floodgate. Somehow, desperately, I hope that what is tumbling out will do, will spontaneously link itself to a form, that the torrent will merge into a wave, that emotion, intellect, psyche and language will gel, in some Dadaesque way, and if I just keep writing, art will happen. But I know it isn't true: and as the sun leaves the cloud, and my shadow in the garden falls on the paper of this jotter, where I write in pale blue, I glance at the excesses and indulgence. I sense an inchoate truth between the lines, but I refuse its call, and let the whole thing stand. I don't have the courage for it, as Al throws pinecones at me from the bedroom window, and a fly hovers over my page and the loaded pen. My writer's eyes are stopped up, although I see the bright daisies standing before me, and the brittle curling leaf from last year's apple trees lying lightly on the cool grass by my liver-spotted hand. Leaves scutter down the path in an urgent sudden breeze, but I lie back on the grass, looking through the branches at the intensely blue sky.

He joins me, singing in his sandals.

I know I cannot do it: I cannot muster the will.

I go to village meetings about policy changes at the local hospital; Al phones me every night, and I write his words in shorthand in my diary, and to amuse myself, juxtapose them with those entries of my own.

'.....she's an actress friend of Paul's. Just a peripheral person to me. She might stay the night - yes, I suppose she will. We've been drinking beer and smoking joints. But she'll be off at the crack of dawn - she's got rehearsals.'

'The black river, swollen and rushing high under the little bridges on the way to the sea at night after torrential rain - next day it's fallen to a normal level, and sparrows fly from branch to branch of the birch and elm trees above.'

'The kids thought my new tie was silk. I bought cough sweets and shampoo and did the supermarket shopping. I'm giving up smoking on Wednesday.'

'The rocks are black, as well as the stream: there's a symmetry between wave and stone, up and up the river, as far as the eye can see - you could leap from rock to rock, over the silent white foam; just enough of them: just the right size.'

'Yes, I'm giving up ciggies for good tomorrow. And being pure: eating a thousand vitamins a day. I miss you and I love you.

You sound a bit more jolly tonight.'

I go shopping myself, and in the supermarket, I watch the soft eyes of the inmates of the hospital. They hold the hand of the nurse in charge, and gaze in rapture at beans and bananas, muttering personal mantras, smiling, dribbling, crying. Some stride, clubfooted, down the pavements, intent on letter-posting or gardening, their greatest threat to the community merely incontinence or simple-mindedness.

There is a meeting planned, in opposition to the proposed extension of the hospital, to include a medium-secure unit for the criminally insane - there has been a mild furore amid the *nouveau-riche*, the intelligentsia, the tourist association couple, the Liberal councillor, the café owner from the prom, the hospital union man.

"We don't want rapists and murderers wandering about, do we?"

And, despite my mother's exhortations to take the 'tide in the affairs of men' at its flood, to tell Al to stay away while I write, to take my work seriously, I write only desultorily.

She is preparing for a second eye operation.

"It has to be done," she tells me today, recalling how the problem started, with 'everything gradually losing colour, and very slowly becoming duller' until the cataract was removed, the vision refreshed, and that vital ability to differentiate tone and colour restored, so that she could paint again.

When we were small and my dad was cartooning, my mother asked if she could learn how to draw. He made her a pencilled grid over photographs in the *National Geographic*, and she copied out for herself the scenes of irrigation plants or giraffe-necked women.

In these recent years, when he was resting in the afternoons, she'd gone to art classes with her friend, June, or they'd worked in each other's homes on their watercolour still lifes and picture postcard views.

Now, while she waits to go to hospital, she asks me to draw the pictures for her, and I sit at the polished table in her living room, sketching out her favourites, from the colour supplements or birthday cards, of swans and sunsets, little girls playing - 'Like you and Lottie, I thought'- doves strutting in courtyards, boats on canals, peacocks, medieval streets with tumbling architecture and picturesque corners of farm kitchens.

"Look at that," she still says, if we're out walking, and she points to a piece of groundsel poking heroically up though a crack in the pavement.

I envy her the charm she finds here, as I do her unsophisticated choice of subject: the trouble she takes to perfect a bird's wing or the bridge's reflection in the water.

"You wouldn't see me for dust if I'd had your chances," she tells me, dipping her sable brush into a jar of water.

"Can't you take him more lightly? Just bounce him along by your side like a balloon?"

"I wish I could."

"Do you think it's her age?" I hear her asking Lottie, when I am supposedly out of earshot. "Is she worried about getting to be fifty?"

Lottie is diplomatic in her reply: never overtly critical of me, because perhaps she needs me to be as strong and sure as when I had busily marched to the front of the class, with the dinner-money.

"I'm going to make sure I don't make the same mistakes as you."

She had been alarmed at my secret letters from Liverpool, and at the disintegration of my marriage. Once she brought a friend to visit us, who gazed in awe at the evidence of our arty married life.

"I love these pottery dishes," the girl said, fingering the rough surfaces, eyes widening at our bohemianism: the cot in the corner with its Klee painting; the painted station clock; the sculptures on the sideboard; the splashes of blood on the wall, where Frank had cut his hand when sweeping them off in a rage.

Lottie married a man who fell ill and became unenthusiastic, then nurseryman Tom, who proved ungovernable. Now she lives with Charles, a farmer, and her teenage daughter Amy: and twenty-six year old Juliet, who is pregnant.

At Charles' house in Snowdonia, Al learns how to milk the goat, obediently doing what he is told, acquiescing subtly to a notion of our worldliness and his näiveté, always discovering new things to learn , and discreetly refusing equality. We're the ones with mortgages, children, ageing parents, histories and blunders. His life is spread out like a frozen pond in the morning sun, shimmering and enticing and empty.

I stand in the rushes, at the edge of this chilling expanse, leaning towards those glassy panes, under which I sense nourishment and salvation, but not quite hungry enough to delve yet, and not quite able.

'We'll have a café with a speciality for schoolkids: sausages, but grilled. And as much tea as you can drink for ten pence extra. Are there any other cafés in the village?'

'Watching that swirling sand - it almost drowns out the memory of the danger of walking out there, towards the sea, when those little flood rivers are filling up and fattening out and could block the way back.'

'It's having no nicotine - I go crazy: too much oxygen. It's withdrawal symptoms. It does affect the libido - it doesn't mean I've lost my desire for you.'

'Astonishing crimson sky at dusk, through the black silhouettes of the trees in the wood- then over the estuary, opposite, lilac streaks turning to cool, pale blue, and neon-green street lights and cars flickering from the island - all reflected in the wet sands and the thin currents: the air still and fine like ice.'

'Definitely it's the holiday that's made you feel that way. But there's no need. I love you.'

TALK TO ME

The blue face of the Timex watch my dad bought me for Sicily glowed at me, as I sat writing my diary in the dusk, in a corner of the Syracuse Express in Rome.

In that same book today, above the pencilled notes on my Communist friend, I find two poppies pressed, delicately transparent, and faded to a bloodless, yet calm violet. They were a vivid vermilion when I picked them, shot through with sunlight. Enzo had driven in the heat with the car windows closed, climbing the road up the barren hillside. Giangaetano, who studied English with us, waved from his scooter as he flew down towards the car, and when we stopped, and Enzo read his newspaper, I climbed out to pick the scant flowers, hearing him decline Giangaetano's offer of dinner with the melancholy young widow, Francesca: he would see me afterwards.

A butterfly snagged its legs in the thick linen tablecloth, in the restaurant at the military base in Catania. Giangaetano stretched the skin over my hand and told me it was green: I must be from Betelgeuse. Francesca would not be flirted with by the American servicemen at another table, smiling at me with a small lipstick mark on her teeth, yet giving me, as the lawyer did, a glimpse of those who had gained mastery over their lives, and for whom no shadowy, impatient figure waited at the end of the street for his bluff to be called.

On Saturday mornings, in the cool marble-floored living room, when the family was out, I would sit writing, under the masks from Africa nailed to the walls. I was as odd a trophy, with my thick tights and bleached hair: the children took me for rides on their scooters, and the adults arranged dates for me, where I ate cheese-stringy *aranciatas,* mumbled high-flown observations on hypocrisy and love, and watched the prostitutes of Syracuse as my driver shouted insults.

I pointed out Wales on the map of Britain in my classes, and lingered on the cities, while my son set off for his new school in Liverpool.

I talked about London buses and the Beatles: in the text books we looked at pictures of Nelson's Column and other monuments, heaped at their bases with foreign students like themselves: I glanced at the wall at last year's exam results, and the signature 'Iris Roberts, *Insegnante*'.

Soon I was using the dialect of my host family and my pupils: eager with phrases like '*Parra co' mea*', instead of '*Parla con me,*' when I wanted to chat. It was as fascinating as when I learned French at school, scrawling '*l'apostrophe*' in delight, across bus timetables on the way home.

Life chased past; the outlying schools in poor towns that I went to by bus, past scrawny cattle, and lizards, and lemon trees; the unexpected snowy peak of Etna rising from a smoky cloud; cobbled streets with wooden-faced women in doorways; smells of nuts and sardines, the curled-iron balconies where washing blew; rain falling in torrents from gutterless roofs. And, in a shop of sugar-violet Easter eggs, with writer's eyes, I was suddenly free of attachments and closer to essences, aware of something uncanny and potent, exciting the nerves and the eyes and the intelligence: a cold thing, but alive and trembling and strange. I dawdled there, by a glass cabinet full of chocolate eggs, smelling the fading scent of mimosa, then turned for school, where the girls and boys waited on the steps, and I cleaned the board from the last lesson, and, with a fresh piece of chalk, wrote the date in English.

The artist who could have fluttered into being in that old and provocative land lay unmoved - not for her Arethusa's fountain with its water to cure freckles; the Carthaginian Wars; the catacombs; the forum and arena, the amphitheatre; dishes of eels; clumps of papyrus. She was still, emotionally, a woman in a Welsh village, simpering and flattering, and waiting for love.

"Just imagine if we walked round the corner and there was Rhos!"

Seb had come to join me, and we walked on those dusty white roads, as I exhorted him to rejoice in the newness, the magic, the superiority of the place over our own. In orange groves, I taught him English Literature for the exam he would sit at home, while, in the distance, NATO warships gathered for the Afghanistan war. While analysing Wordsworth's 'Michael', we planned to depart, if necessary, on the motorbike I bought him, with the thousands of lire stashed in my drawer.

I close the diary, with its purplish flat flowers, its tightly-written script, and a programme for the performance of *The Bacchae*, illustrated with a drawing of the wild-haired Maenads. The sun floats on, now halfway through a brindled cloud. I smell the cigarette end which Al has just stubbed out in his ashtray: six inches away his toes curl in his Countryman socks (built to last), while the television drones on to itself in the house. We talk into the night, then he sings as I try to read, sleeps and snores while I lie fretting, exhausted by discussions of the future, and the sleepy promises I extract from him in the light of the congealing dawn.

Yet he makes the breakfast, goes to the shops, washes the dishes: eyes aghast in apprehensiveness at my erratic speeches, boyishly making himself scarce with his novel, so I can get on with my writing...and the sun disappears behind a thicker piece of mackerel; marigolds smoulder in abrupt orange smudges among lilac streaks of loosestrife and the stiff hydrangeas in my borders.

"Write," said friends, when I ask their advice.

"Write," I say to myself.

"Make marmalade," says D. H. Lawrence.

"Make tomato chutney - I've got an Indian recipe, with a piece of ginger the size of your fist: cardomoms and chilli peppers and five cloves of garlic. Or paint a Flemish picture of a sailing ship, heading for the Zuyder Zee," says Fred.

But lately he hasn't been painting: his mother has been moved to the nursing home. I go there with him, and we sit in the lounge, in a row of armchairs facing the television.

"This is what she's waiting for," he tells me, pouring a large slug of whisky into her pale tea, as she turns in bleary, greedy satisfaction to where Fred vaguely is.

"They don't give a shit," he nods towards the staffroom, while the television drowns out weak demands, and someone knocks an ashtray off the table and its contents onto the floor. A bustling carer enters, observes, then reappears with a dustpan and brush, as the sound increases with the advertisements, and Fred pours more whisky.

Then I meet him at the crematorium, where he stands in a rented suit, with his ex-wife and four children. I ask him how he is.

"Well. I'm OK, aren't I? It was a shock, I suppose. Bizarre, with the DSS people and the funeral money. They're going to dock it from my Giro now. I haven't heard from Ronnie - he says exports are down - he's buggered off somewhere sunny, I suppose. The boys in the DSS office don't seem to care if I sell any pictures. Can you credit it? 'Don't bother declaring it, Mr. James: you just get on with your art!' It's all mad, isn't it? It's absurd. It's fucking hilarious, really. You just have to disengage. Completely."

"You still care about the kids, though? "

"Of course. But as far as love goes, I've made the same stupid mistakes as you. I mean, look at me and Eunice, here. Would you think we'd ever been married and had these four? She thinks she's the only one who's suffered - she hardly even looks at me. You could write a book. You just wonder what makes you do the things you do, when you sit back later and scratch your head and it's so patently fucking stupid. Something must be skewed for you to make these mistakes. One, I mean."

I look round at the disappearing stragglers. It is the same place we came to with the body of my dad.

"It's only now."

When I was off school once, I rode with him at the front,

upstairs, on a double-decker bus, while he was visiting clients: as we jolted up mountain highways, he explained his theories: "Life is like this scene you can see through this window. It's only what is happening here, in this frame - now. There's nothing before it, or after it, or around it: it's just this."

We were confused by his oblique treatises on The Eternal Now, finding it difficult to live without emotion or ambition or anticipation, and muddled about what seemed to be of more real and practical importance to him - the respect for order, routine, shiny shoes and toeing the line.

At home we fed the hens and waited for them to lay, sitting on a corrugated tin roof with our daisy chains, while our dad leaned against the chicken-wire fence and smoked his cigarette. In the summer holidays, we found day-old chicks scattered on our eiderdown. He taught us with our friends to swim: we stayed in the water until our fingers were shrivelled, and the tide had flowed and ebbed. In term-time, when we were small, our freshly-whitened pumps would be waiting for us for school in the mornings. We lived the humble, traditional working-class life; we watched him do his football pools, and check them on Saturdays; he built a rockery and a trellis for our council house home. On Sunday mornings, we walked in our best clothes with him to his allotment, where we podded sweet-tasting peas. We took holidays by train to grandma in Oldham, where we played on the tip with our cousins, or to grandpa's in Derbyshire, where we ran across the yard at bedtime to the chemical lavatory.

He told us trust the authorities, and we learned a conventional morality, sifted from his army upbringing. We heard soldier's stories of India: he had travelled to Bombay as a teenager with his brother Gerald, and lived rough with natives who loved the 'Ashruf-sahibs'.

He sang us army songs: 'Pack up your troubles', and 'Bye-bye, blackbird', in a deep baritone voice, suffused with his characteristic lugubriousness: his favourites were the old, sentimental ballads, or aching laments, or 'Clementine'.

When Gerald died, he went into the bathroom for a long

time, and never spoke of him again.

The summer before his own death, my father sat in the grounds of the hospital, looking weathered and gentle and ironic, in his pyjamas, moving a stick to make circles in the gravel, and he told me that nothing matters.

"Why do we have to do this? He's only dead."

The long march: the smallest grandchild; the mother, on the arm of the fishing friend in the dark night before Christmas, winding down in a cortège to the shore, where the sea ran in the ebbing tide in the damp air, where ashes were thrown in the wind and across the seas a wave pulled back, and Seb wrote the cherished nickname in the wet sand, before the waters slipped over the letters in dragging bubbles, popping and shining in easy tumult of nature.

Jock, a fisherman and my dad's oldest mate, stood on the beach in the lamplight from the promenade, and the wet wall shone - the place where we spent the summers of our childhood, where Lottie was pushed aside for me to scramble to safety, where we swam in the sea with the father whose ashes now float and dissolve in the perpetuum and distillation of the essence, and propagation of the effect, as in a word or a memory or a seedling from a dandelion clock.

And we stood in our own buddhahood, at our separate, individual points on the graph.

Al paces about in front of the cricket: he plans a weekend trip to Yorkshire to see his family, and I will go to London to see Seb.

I guess that Al will be getting drunk, smoking dope and meeting new women, just as he did at college. My criticisms remain silent, however, because we will, perhaps, be going to look for a place to live in the summer holidays....

"There will be money difficulties, but, if I get this job, we can start living here together in the autumn."

I want to see the British Museum, and seek out the

manuscripts of Virginia Woolf, James Joyce and Charles Dickens. Years ago I read their books, equipped with only a flustered adolescent apprehension, missing any enlightenment or education from *To the Lighthouse, Great Expectations,* or *Ulysses.* But now I know and recognise the hysteria of scribbling down a thought, and the absolute necessity of changing a word here or there: I understand those handwritten corrections, and am reconciled to the idiocy of the effort. What difference does it make, indeed? Where are Mrs Dalloway and Stephen Daedalus now? And Molly Bloom - and Leonard Woolf and Nora Barnacle? Little Nell and Jock the fisherman? We are all a fiction! T. S. Eliot drones on about Ezra Pound and ends and beginnings, marries disastrously and crosses out words of poems, and so do I. Virginia Woolf fills her cardigan pockets with stones, fears incipient madness - I fill mine with caramels and am counselled. Charles Dickens comes to Anglesey as a journalist one day: me, too; and regards the human condition as now comic, now tragic; *anch'io*.

But above the case's glass cover I feel as starkly separate as, pregnant in Derbyshire, from my bedroom window I sketched my aunt's hen-pen, built on a slanted wooded acre.

Those drawings were as fragmented as my world, with their bits of unconnected branch, odd leaves and scattered pencil marks.

I walked the hills with my aunt, after her teaching day was over, and we discussed what to do, as we stamped the bracken.

From the family's point of view, the expectation was of my entering a home for unmarried mothers, or getting married.

"Do you love him?"

"I've nothing to compare it with."

In the tartan maternity dress I'd worn for months, I wed my artist husband at a register office ceremony in Chapel-en-le-Frith, the day after President Kennedy was assassinated, then travelled with him in a rented van, to his parents' home in Wrexham.

Seb and I walk along the streets of vegetable stalls, and small dark shops, with their fruits, and packs of joss-sticks and honey cakes: towards the golden architecture around the Park where he lives. A meal is being prepared for us in the blue kitchen of a house where I will bed down on a leather sofa whose cushions will spring out from under me through the night, as traffic hums outside, and sycamore dangles, and ivy entwines the stone balustrades. I see gardeners tend the earth between bedding plants, picking up a petal or a twig. Fountains spill down the smooth bronze torsos of nymphs and young gods; new walks are being made and old ones renewed, bordered and stilled.

In a patch of hollyhocks, a cat presses stalks, as she languishes and frolics in the sunshine. A hundred yards away is Diorama, amid the stately crescent buildings, so distant from the lawns and loosestrife behind me, where Frank now has his studio, travelling in daily from the outskirts, from Ruth, and three-year-old Martin, to this workroom of eleven-by-eight-foot canvases.

We enter the white painted corridor, and knock on Frank's door.

Seb sits on a sofa-bed inside the studio, and I perch on the arm, sniffing the air.

"It smells exactly like Wrexham - the life room!" I cry, as the vision of paintbrushes that you must clean properly, standing in a jar on a turps-stained newspaper, presents itself to my left.

Ahead of us, Frank is changing from his painting clothes into a clean tee-shirt and trousers. Against the wall stand three of his latest works: linked areas of feathery or thickly-layered paint, swooning or balancing in lakes of carmine or cerulean blue.

Seb comments on the recurrence of a broken line or cord in one of the paintings, which they both promptly christen *Umbilicus*. I've donated titles, too, in the past: kings-in-the-altogether like *Hamartia*, or *Hubris*, or *Nemesis*.

Now we regard the work in silence, except for the odd utterance from each, and are united familially, lapsed in memories and the curiousness of creation. Frank speaks in puzzled tones, as always, about what he is doing: never sure, and never finished with it.

"The line just takes me with it - it goes where it wants, and

I don't know what's going to happen."

We look at another picture: wide bands of violet host many bustling forms: we three survey in silence the work of the lad who walked the Aggie, and I breathe nostalgia and unhappiness with the smell of oil and turps, longing for the lost girl who wrote in a shoebox lid that she was nineteen, while this man, stepping out of his paint-spattered pants, and self-consciously pulling on clean clothes, arrived on that birthday at her flat, with a bunch of red tulips held behind his back.

We sit in the white air, Seb's eyes blue; Frank's hazel like mine; the ceruleans, viridians, magentas and cobalts shimmering in sympathy, splintering off into shafts from the central white light: red, orange, yellow, blue, indigo, green, violet.....somewhere, over the rainbow....... he takes the line or the line takes him then we stroll in a row down Oxford Street to tea and goodbyes: Seb and I on the bus in sudden thundery rain, and Frank off to his hinterland home.

"I'd like a game of pinball - let's have a pint," says my son, so we jump off to run across the road into a pub where stained glass lights fall upon the tables in a burst of sunshine through the showers, and I look round from my stool, while Seb obliterates family and art, in the disinterested bagatelle of bulbs and coarse illustrations, curved tunnels and bulging scores.

A group of men are ordering food nearby: I can smell new potatoes, and I hear an American voice: "*Dels*? Oh, Des! Sit yourself down, Des," inviting a local with a plastic carrier bag to join them as the waitress approaches.

"Mustard? Sauce? No?"

She moves away in her plum-coloured short skirt.

A moment later she is back, with a plate of bread and butter - sliced bread and margarine - and a dumpy man in a teal-coloured shirt eats a piece, while his neighbour scratches the top of his head.

The American voice, talking about Ireland, has reached fever pitch: "We'll buy you a beer, Des."

Des, poised for departure, clutches the back of a chair and his plastic bag with the same hand.

A gingerhaired man piles peas on his fork as the sun lights up the back of his head.

O father, you were right, in your buddhahood and sansara, and have no need to resume the circle, and return to the wheel of suffering and desire.

WHITE PATHS

Where through arcs of aching light
I searched
And kept looking.

"Come on - we're celebrating your bursary!"

Rosa, through whose agency I'd found work in Greece, is here in London, interviewing teachers for the islands and mainland.

Ten years ago, in pink dungarees, she stood across the table to interview me for the job in Piraeus: on the walls were pinned posters of the stark white buildings and humming blue skies of Kos, Skiathos, and Brenda Chamberlain's Hydra.

"It'll be better for you to be near to Athens, than on the islands in winter - more things to do."

I hadn't known what or where she was talking about, privately promising to jog around the Acropolis instead of the wet Welsh lanes, and earn a living for myself, jointly funding Seb's college course with Frank, by then in London.

I started work in October, at the Metsis School of English, in Nikea, in deepest, oldest Piraeus.

As the plane descended, I looked down at an unlovely landscape, where all seemed ridged and inhospitable, and, seamlessly on from the last entry on my life in Wales, wrote *Hellas* and the date.

"Hello, darling! You look very glam!"

Rosa was suddenly upon me, and, before the next group

arrived, took me to see my school and meet the boss.

"They're a bit shit-hot with the grammar, and they love the old drills. Is that OK?"

I needed to look no further than the dog-eared and badly-written text-books, with densely-described points of grammar, to see what I was getting into: my heart sank at the gratuitous exceptions to rules, printed in bold type, and the erratic repetitions of arcane phrases.

The Metsis School was housed in a high-rise concrete building, on the main road to Athens: my two-roomed flat lay at the top of eight or nine flights of stairs, where a life-sized cardboard Beefeater stood at each turn. Mr Metsis was sweatily dapper, in a dark, double-breasted suit, impressed with his Englishness, and the Union Jacks pinned to every wall.

"You will enjoy furnishing your little home!" he beamed, unlocking the heavy door to usher me into a small living space, with louvred windows, a single bed tucked into the corner, and a highly-polished mahogany table in the centre of the mezzanine floor.

From the balcony, he waved his arm at the Acropolis, then was careful to show me how the time-switches worked, and how to lock the heavy front door: I would be alone in the building, when the school day was over - leaning over the rail, with a can of beer, to look at the floodlit wonders of the Athens night, isolated but for the muted sounds of a family behind the concrete wall, next door.

"You'll be fine here!" Rosa said.

I marvelled at this bilingual woman, who single-handedly placed teachers in schools all over Greece, who interviewed and signed people up and arranged flights and insurance and had a shipping merchant lover and an Athens flat. But at the party she threw there for the new contingent, it was clear I had left nothing behind, in terms of the bourgeois convention. Gangling young men in specs, spotty jet-lagged women with swollen ankles, in Marks & Spencer shorts, appropriated her phone to reassure Auntie Madge in Pontefract that they'd arrived and were in safe hands. They clustered in the room, their *raisons d'être* clanging loudly round their heads: celebrating the Greek Experience, and their departure from the norm, before returning those brief arrows of daring to their perpetual lodging, in the heart of the English system they had temporarily quit.

I chatted with Rosa in her kitchen: she joked about consciousness-raising feminist friends, and asked me about my love life.

"Oh, I was going out with someone before I came out here. Much younger than I am."

My life, in contrast with that of this woman of such initiative and independence, seemed hollow. Her man, she told me, was married.

It was fine; it suited her; they had been together for years.

"But I want his child. And nothing seems to happen. I thought it was something I had some sort of choice over!"

And here I befriended thirty-year-old Phoebe, who would organise our café meetings, and the trips I'd never have attempted alone. While I stared gloomily at the Coke cans on Sounion beach, wondering about Shelley or Byron, Phoebe would train her expensive camera on pale, rare plants, telling me that she'd abandoned suburbia and boyfriend for just this freedom.

"I don't want those things at home. I want something extraordinary - I want to be exotic!"

We mooched around the Parthenon in the sun. I picked up a stone, and offered it to her as a souvenir.

"I don't think we're supposed to take even little bits away," Phoebe cautioned, as we sat in the shade at the roadside.

"The stone reminds me of Siddhartha - have you read the book?"

"Mmm. Heard of it, I think. What happens? Why the stone?"

"Siddhartha was the son of a Brahmin. But he was unhappy - he thought that no one understood the truth about life."

"What - all the rituals and religion didn't add up?"

"That's right. He left his family, and with his friend, Govinda, joined a band of ascetics, who had renounced the flesh."

"Did that work?"

"No. He realised he couldn't escape his own self, whatever

he put himself through to lose it."

"So?"

"He and Govinda heard about Gotama, the Buddha, who had the secret, apparently, so off they went to see for themselves."

"Left the ascetic ones for good?"

"Yes, and found the Buddha and listened to his teachings, and Govinda decided that this was for him."

"But not old Siddhartha?"

"No. Not then, anyway."

"Why? And what were the teachings of the Buddha, anyway?"

"The Buddha said that everything in the world is connected: it is all one. And everything in the world contains the buddha-nature."

"Even a stone."

"Yes."

"He said that we suffer because of what he called our attachment to things - our desires. If we could overcome desire and attachment, we would find peace, and not have to reincarnate to learn the lesson."

"Sounds OK to me. What didn't Siddhartha like about that?"

"He did like it, and he accepted the teachings. He agreed that the world is a whole, a unity, with everything connected. But he told the Buddha that though he knew he was right, he, Siddhartha, could not experience another's enlightenment - he said that nobody attains salvation just through teachings."

"Even the Buddha's? It would have done for me!"

"Siddhartha had to find out for himself. So he had lots of adventures, and finally came to see for himself what the Buddha said: all is indeed one in the world, and he understood, too, that sorrows have to be concluded, or they must be lived through again. When he was an old man, he met Govinda again, and showed him how the division between things is really an illusion."

"So if there's no division between things, there's no time, either, I suppose?"

Yes - no past, present or future. Only now. Here, take it."

I gave Phoebe the stone, and we walked down the white paths towards the city.

I was working in a school ruled by spurious standards and attainments, in a place where traffic screamed day and night beneath my room; where I sat on my rooftop balcony, trying to decipher the cyrillic letters chalked on the wall of the building opposite. *Demokratia* may have burst into being, as the varnish peeled off my cheap wooden chair in the relentless sunshine, but nothing else was spelt out for me under the acres of blue that fell back into further shimmering and silent realms. In solitude, I sat in the throbbing light, with eyes closed.

I tried on new shoes on rainy Saturdays in my room in Piraeus, listening to the sounds of the family next door: I had no idea of who they might be, sensing a movement sometimes on their balcony, or seeing the washing put out to dry.

I was trapped in a world where I made no difference; where the tumult of visitors treading the floor of history beat irritatingly and futilely day after day; where planes fell like Icarus in a joke of civilisation and control, minute on minute; where Plaka stallholders made evil curses when I didn't buy a scarf or a ring: all seemed hot and grey and refusing; with life and its baggage sliding across the surface of the world like buildings across a seismic shudder: all seemed disposable and rootless and irrelevant, like the floating twigs on the Derbyshire trees which, savage and excluded, I had drawn in pregnancy. I was in love with no one, too intimidated by the city to relax into the old neurosis: on red alert for pirates and pickpockets and cut-throats, numbed into submission by the tracelessness and cluelessness of the place: physically and psychically lost amid the huge ships nudging the harbour wall, their fading names gleaming through rusty tracks down their massive bows.

Here hung at night the stars of Orion, locked in eternal relationship with earth and the other star groups, but leaning at a different angle now, in a disturbing corner of the sky - the same constellation I'd looked at and loved from my little back bedroom in Wales, when Seb was tucked up, to shout goodnight.

I met other foreigners, ate in quayside restaurants, and took the ferry to Aegina and Hydra, but those islands seemed toylike and Disneyesque to me, as I drank with Phoebe and Greek sailors in their bars, or climbed their flowered terraces, or whirled back to Athens in their hydrofoils.

I failed to return at the first Christmas, and when I had convinced Rosa of the reason, she packed up my diaries and Greek rugs, and used the drachmas under the bed to send them on, while I turned again to a man for love.

Lightly and easily I swapped those Hydra tavernas for a Jobcentre in Grimweave Street, the Metsis School for Clacton Heath Comprehensive; the view of the Parthenon for a flat sky and a corner shop; taramasalata for fish fingers; my faded jeans for the brightly-napped cashmere coat; what I thought was loneliness for what I thought was love.

"I need you," said the telephone engineer, when I stepped off the plane.

He bit his nails until they bled: he told me that his house would be mine: he would help me find a job.

"Think about shaking the snow off your shoes in winter on my doormat. Think about going to Southwold to camp; think about Aldeburgh."

"Is he going to marry you?" asked Fred.

"You don't want to work in a school in Harwich, do you, Mum?" asked nineteen-year-old Seb.

I phoned Rosa, who thought I had planned this, and Phoebe, who thought I was mad, and the black-suited Mr Metsis, who was very cross, and went to Harwich.

And for a time I lived with Ray, in his modern brick house, dodging the punk lodger's hairdryer to put the kettle on.

I waited at the squash club, drinking beer while he checked the league tables.

He cooked our meals, and we sat at the table eating unsalted vegetables.

He did the washing and ironing, and watched *Dallas*, with

his legs hanging over the arm of the chair.

He turned the heating off when he left for work.

When I broke a heavy glass lampshade with my volley, and cut my nose while practising squash in his boxroom, he told me to lie down and be careful not to get blood on the duvet.

I watched him park his car at six o'clock every evening, and run in and pull his bullworker from under the bed and do his exercises.

After some weeks, he told me it was costing him a lot to have me there: the lodger would have to stay.

When I tried to write my book, he scattered the manuscript across the floor and said it was trash.

When I applied for work and didn't get it, he said, "No wonder - you've got a career history as long as your arm."

'Where I was made ridiculous
By sharp-bladed life......'

After three years, in which I worked as a full-time English teacher, we broke up. During my arrangements to move north to a new job, my dad died.

Rosa, a lone parent now, pours champagne.

I return to my empty cottage, and to my despondent, ambivalent life.

I pick up my apples from the grass, and see how quickly the slugs have got to them.

I pay my bills and put an extra sweater on in the cool evenings.

I call my mother every evening at six.

I walk to the public meeting in the community centre, where villagers angrily confront the authorities about the projected building of the medium-secure unit.

I think about my love affair, and what to do.

I remember how, when I first knew him, Al would call at my house in his running shorts, and sit down on a pile of ironing, and talk and joke, or winningly quote from John Donne or Keats, or *Omar*.

I realise I've been bullying him into commitment, and must acknowledge the fact.

"I've been wrong to force your hand, Al. I understand your difficulty in considering a life together."

How can he have been at fault? He has travelled to see me as often as he can, even while keeping me at arm's length from his new friends: he has telephoned me every day and loved me, as far as I know, faithfully, throughout his teacher training and his first years of work.

Instead of student escapades these days, I hear of classroom successes, and how the kids laugh at his remarks, and matrons my own age blush.

He is not a bad man, and we have talked and laughed and cooked and spent many contented hours together. I believe in his qualities of honour, humility and kindness, just as I see he is, as I am, thoughtless and insecure: his faults are inescapably merely those of immaturity.

If blame lies anywhere, I decide, it lies with me, for not recognising or admitting to myself my own needs for a partner who can identify appropriately with my life.

Yet Al insists this was his aim in applying for the job near me: he still says he wants us to be together, and for us to make beer from the butcher's kits, buy second-hand furniture and paint and mend the house.

I complained about his collar stiffeners in my hearth, on the day of the interview, yet I had been alight with joy at the prospect of a life with him: painting still-lifes and imagining dinner parties, just as when I married Frank.

In the light of his stated intentions, then, even though he failed in his job application and has made no more, and we have dredged once more through the unlikely and desultory considerations of my living and working with him, can't I, once and for all, throw the cards in the air?

Why not make the ultimate decision for us both, accepting and loving him for what he is?

Why not face it out and take him aboard, wholesale, with his obliviousness and his tenderness and his curries and his third-form registers?

What else do I have and who else do I want and what do I think is going to be different?

Why isn't it enough, just being loved? I still need the living love, more than what might be.

I decide we will have one last try.

Tearfully and emotionally, I phone him at his parents' in Yorkshire.

"I know I said I wouldn't nag you any more about commitment, but I just mean I'd rather get on with things together, with living it, whatever is involved," I say, meaning it.

My heart is bursting by now: I have burned myself up with working it out: this is a final, flailing gesture.

"Are you sure you're not just saying that? You won't have changed your mind by tomorrow?"

"I promise," I answer, moistly.

"Good," breathes my hero, and we both laugh.

ANNIHILATION

'*Where a full-bloodied knife*
Tore my hope to ribbons
Which wave in my fear'

In the humid morning when I wake, I hear birdsong.

I see from the window the tall horse chestnut in the wood opposite.

The old tree stands black and green in a grey mist, and I listen to the soft distant sound of rain water, falling from gutters to iron grids. Birds fly past, like people with their shopping in the village streets, quickly across my field of vision and into the trees, vanishing among the nodes where young grass-green conkers hang.

I stand in the open doorway of my house, where a rain-sodden maidenhair fern in the near corner of the garden shimmers with drops of water that seem to pierce like stars the leaf fabric, in gold and ice-blue and emerald, rose, orange and white, and growing more rich as the sun bursts through a film of cloud, complementing the blue-green foliage with a pulse of natural light, augmenting and dramatising in a thrill of simplicity and silent accolade: stained-glass speckles in the maidenhair. When the sun goes behind a cloud again, the droplets show still, now in subtly beautiful pearl and silver.

"So, it's on at last! About to take up the reins of your life!"

Fred is ironic and cautious.

"I'm taking the chance."

"Ah! 'The gold-leafed grail that shimmers, past the breadbin where the loaf lies, and the wineglass glimmers'....! What - is he moving in?"

"We'll have to discuss it. But I'm getting the house fixed up, and I'm going to learn to drive."

"Very commendable. Well, we're all separate individuals with free will. If you think this is the answer, then good luck."

The nights seem short and the dawns early; this week, Earth passes through the tail of a comet; shooting stars are everywhere in the atmosphere; showers of carbon fall, and there is a gratuitous beauty to the fleeting night skies of late summer; daytime decisions float to the ground, sparkling and superfluous as these bursts of mysterious hail; one moves heavily in one's own sphere, caught by the wrist, pausing to remember the reason, sensing and fearing it, and quivering in unsleeping silence, watching for the sun.

In a suitcase in my bedroom sit the diaries I've fretted and fumed in for so long. Across page after page lies the snail-trail of dependency and dread, that the powerful other - now Al, in the past the Kafka X or Y - might denounce me. It's sad to see the acres of green ink and blue biro bruising the white-lined paper, the tedious incidence of 'he', and the self-conscious use of shorthand when all becomes too humiliating.

The telephone rings: it is Al.

I want to know what he's been doing: his tone is strained and polite as he tells me he's been walking on the moors with his philosopher father.

"He slipped and fell into the bog."

He laughs nervously, then launches into an erratic discourse.....

"Wittgenstein ... *agape* ... *eros* ... I'm really a nihilist ...I've always been one ... and...um ... it doesn't affect my love for you, but it's...it's in the light of that..."

And he talks of how 'blithe' he used to be, and has now become 'obsessive' and is causing himself misery; he's brought himself down.

"Since being with me, you mean?"

"I don't know."

"What are you getting at, Al?"

"I'm not sure."

My heart trembles.

"How do you really feel about things?"

"I'm not sure."

"What about us?"

"I don't know."

The words drop from my lips.

"Do you want us to finish?"

"Yes."

"You want that?"

"Yes."

Silence lies between us for a few seconds.

I hear his breath and remember his thoughtful ways: this good, *homme moyen sensuel*, who licks the tears from my nose when I cry, has ceased to love me: he has seen me for what I am, and has rejected it: the unimaginable has come to pass at last.

Hours later I crawl to the edge of the bed and look out at the bowl of night, at the flurries of star and aerolite, until the dawn illuminates the room. From the mirror, my own bone-white face stares back. For an hour I remain: to shift my gaze is to dissolve in the stream of meteors.

Next day I go to the beach of my childhood: past the places where I'd lived as a girl; peeping through slatted fences at the little greenhouse and the long lawn where we had come from school, with ties undone, and berets thrown off the pier, to the sun-warmed home where I was arrogant and happy in my veneer. The sun has come out now, and I walk that same beach where we'd played as children and languished as teenagers, and sit against a rock on the pebbles at the place where we scattered my dad's ashes, and I pray for help. From this beach we'd gone swimming, in the ways my dad taught us, and struggled in and out of our knitted bathing costumes while my mam held a towel round us. We learned the breast-stroke and the crawl, and he would tell us of his lifeguard days with Gerald, when they worked at Southport swimming baths, and on the great swathes of beaches at Ainsdale.

"We swam every day, and in the evenings used to sit about smoking marijuana, and drinking wine and beer, and reading Zen Buddhism and poetry, with the breeze blowing in soft zephyrs past our ears."

All the kids swam and played with my dad in the water, and my mam, in her skirt and blouse, would be waiting with the towels and picnic: I see her now, with her dark, shoulder-length hair, parted at the side, spreading out the sandwiches and Tizer on a cloth over the stones, while we stood, quivering and round-bellied, dripping rats' tails of hair, waiting for food and warmth.

I pick up a green marble that has become dulled by the sea: I lean against a damp breakwater, smelling the brown seaweed, strong and salty, careful of the sharp, broken barnacles on the white, smoothed wood, fixed in my mac and in my expression and in my attitude: unable to sustain the fragile sense of a future self, fallen once more into horror at the being that can never be loved; reconciling myself to a congealed, isolated fate.

Somehow, I have transgressed missionary law: the Yorkshire elder has pinpointed my irretrievably savage centre before toppling into the bog, warning the acolyte of the danger ahead: at one end of the country a life has been saved for the service while, of necessity, at the other, another has been sacrificed.

Al and I scan a different coastline and a different sea, and I pick up blurred marbles, filling my mac pockets with grey and white pebbles. I will not hear from him, I know: he has made his getaway, despite my controls. He has saved himself, just in time.

My mind bolts like a scalded cat through its restless memories, shamed and burning and exposed: I see Seb, crying in the bath for his daddy at my mother's, his fevered colour and his tearful three-year-old's description of how things seemed to him.

"Like looking into a spoon - everything upside down."

I confront the ocean and the sky and the nauseating self I have finally failed to disguise as good. So, what is left to me?

Mourning is beginning in me; sharp pangs of yearning which I know will sear more deeply soon; I quail at the thought of the next minutes and the bald afternoon to come; heart and stomach are one; a grisly mass of oozing loathing of the clutching, savage child I can never deny.

I find a promenade café, and sit there alone, overlooking the ashy sea.

In front of me stands a vase of vibrant irises: behind me two young homosexual men talk, waiting for customers in the spruce and eager room. Menus and loose advertisements lie on the glass counter where I pay for my drink, before taking out my red and black notebook at the table. I see joggers along the iron railings, and the full, deep ocean swells idly and flaccidly against the constraining sea wall. I try to write, but feel desolate and muddy-minded: I am in a chaos of identitylessness and the sentences are getting me nowhere. Then the irises begin to insist on themselves, on their own papery rich blueness, and I observe an almost-purple bud in front of me. As I stood crying on a chair when I was an infant, and noticed I could make the shafts of light from the electric light bulb stretch and shimmer sideways through my tears, the more I squeezed my eyes, similarly now I'm distracted from my problem, discerning the tightly-sheathed bloom in its verdant case: how yellow clouds the curl of the opening heavenly petal with a passionate anointing lick: it is within inches of me. Beyond, I hear the voices of the gay golden boys among the coffee cups and stems of carnations in glass jars: the hopeful new young proprietor and his friend cast surreptitious glances into the long, gleaming kitchen where the new manager runs for cream for my coffee, and brings it in a blue and white striped jug, all for me, and I must just shout out if I want a fill-up. The vast grey sea lies before me, and tangled in the leafless trees sprouting alongside the wide window, red and faded blue flags of bunting fly.

The edge of the land is always a good place: the harbour at Hydra, where the white houses astound on the terraced rocks; the paddling in hot evenings in the broad clear waves of the coast of Calabria; the camping in Southwold; the beaches here with Al.

Suddenly, for a moment, I am confused about who has been my partner in each of these places: they seem to have merged into one - identifiable only by their youth and life's promise, and the icy nips of what-might-have-been, still flooding me with pain and bliss of hope like a shot of heroin.

"He only wanted to mark his books and get smashed and go to the pub, and you want to write, mum," says Seb, at my news.

"You were always saying he'd be growing leather patches on his elbows," says Juliet.

"This was your Day One Thousand," Lottie tells me, as we walk with Charles along his lane in the dark, with our arms round each other, under the palpitating broad night sky of a peninsula. We consider the surface realities, the indications for the future. But we all know, sensing the stone patio under our feet, as we sit in nighties and tracksuits, that our inchoate subject has its own esoteric and dynamic, and our analyses, our frowns and smiles, are litter on its fierce voyage through our skies, and, as we flail in the comet's tail, so we are immobile against this other pure purpose.

"Maybe he's helped you to define yourself - maybe this will be good for you. Perhaps he's been your salvation," says Fred, interested.

And I see the irony of it: how, to be completely annihilated, one must be perfectly arranged, at one's most vulnerable: I could not have been more ready for humiliation, and he could not have displayed his power more adroitly. Once again, I have glimpsed my otherness, from where I stand in the shadow of his, and I see how a psychological poison has blighted my nature, like an oil spill whose surface pollution sinks by association to the sand and bone of the old ocean floor.

"You'll be alright by yourself. You don't realise."

Always, the evidence before me, of a single woman living successfully alone, has been one-dimensional: I have refused the grace and substance of this or that drawing or the gift of a painting; blind to the colour of my kitchen walls, vivid with photographed human groupings and reluctant grins; the dancers and boats and wine bottles of any Impressionist scene; the dashes of green and blue grasses and skies I've sat on and walked under with family and friends. I have been ignorant of the words to the prayer I live; intent instead upon fattening the sacrificial lamb with liquorice allsorts, brushing its wool, and collecting dry matches to light the pyre.

Now I sense a sudden peeling-away - a feeling that my candle-flame has shuddered violently and bent to its weak wick root, but is tremulously shining again and steadying. I am stripped but standing: somehow, I have lived on, and this realisation is both of amazement and gratitude: even though I suffer anxiety, I am still there to live it. I have not been annihilated, after all: Al exists still, even as the all-powerful other - but so, too, do I.

So I read again the old quotes from *Literary Women* - phrases which have fired me; lives which have inspired me: female writers centred in themselves and occasional male disguise. Through them, I have discovered how an extreme conciliatoriness is born of dissembling and denial, and I see how the mask and the cloak of the will-less female has begun to suffocate and throttle me. I have been unable to pull on those hard boots and strike sparks from the city cobbles as I stride across them. I have lain, instead, on my belly in the eternally comforting sunshine in a garden on the Welsh coast, with upstairs thousands of words scribbled in exercise books, gazing at the white blossoms of the fragile wind anemones growing in the rockery.

I walk in the lanes as I did when Seb was a schoolboy, seeing the leaves of branches bounding before me: red berries of rowan from the spare little woods. One path winds up to a long avenue of elms, where in spring sheep graze among the rhododendrons, nuzzling their way across tractor tracks above the view of ruckled sands and the thin sideways tides of the Straits. In winter the snow drifts freeze here at the roadsides, sugary and puckered, dredged in wedgy heaps that form themselves into smooth sculptures in the mild drizzle. In summer I've breathed coolness from the hillside bracken, and in springtime looked for the film of green again, conscious of the movement underground and in the leaf-cells, the penetration of light and warmth, the stirrings and renascent swarmings, in yet another season of new-lambs-for-old, and sempiternal daffodils, under dwindling grey skies and cold afternoon-edge.

Al and I have walked here too, talking about poetry, bobbing through the meandering walks like lost tennis balls in a stream: one slightly ahead in the main flood; the other dizzied in jabbering whirlpools. I might have bobbed off into the stream, instead of ploughing a foamy path of wiles and beseeching at his side. Or I might have blinked laconically at those rivers and fields and skies, and whipped out a paintbrush, considering how this or that mix of colour would be most apt, wondering why I hadn't brought a thinner brush; congratulating myself on the stunning composition; thanking God for the shattered sunlight and the branches of hawthorn.

Passing my neighbours' homes on my return, in fine rain, I smell bacon breakfasts: across from me, a thick mist hangs over Anglesey. Cats play under cars as I walk by, and I pick an early blackberry from an overhanging bramble bush. As the fruit melts on my tongue, I notice, in the hedge, some smaller, unripe clusters, and among these, several rusty, browning sepals, where the berry has not developed at all. The tiny, bright green nodules of the unformed blackberry peep out from the leaves, as I crush to powder in my fingers the tobacco-like debris of the failed fruit. I hear the soft scuffle of the animals, as I smell the lingering fragrance of the bacon, and, as the mist lifts slightly, I drag wax crayons on crude drawing paper; make purple roofs with red and blue; dot snowmen's eyes with black coals; run home from school as my ribbon falls out; do sums; cut out princes and princesses. My mam makes stews, and my dad draws; I knit striped bobble hats; I swim; I stand on a chair to read to the inspector, and the milk warms by the coal fire in the classroom.

I rock my sister's pram, as a spectrum of colours falls across her coverlet.

I see the tiny, curling finger of my baby son.

I return home, and phone Al's parents' house.

They are friendly and pleasant.

"He's not here - he's gone to London. He's a law unto

himself, you know. Do you want the number?"

I ring the number in Dulwich, and Al himself answers.

It is good to hear my voice.

A letter is in the post.

He would like to talk things over with me.

Soon.

HARVEST

Touching a raindrop on a fern with my pen, I see how the ink immediately skims into it, lurching and marbled, loading it with deep blue, and it hangs there, blue-burdened irrevocably now, where a moment earlier it was filled with vestal light. I am writing a press release for Frank's next exhibition.

"Could you do it, do you think? I've tried, but Ruth says it sounds pretentious, and the girl at the gallery writes stuff like 'interesting' and 'dramatically different'."

I hold his slides up to the light, remembering the work at his studio. I look down to read the words he has cobbled together: 'While my three-year-old son rises sunflower-like in splendour amid the leafy spaces of Lambeth...' and I recall the Aggie. I shuffle through the pictures, thinking of the flat by the steelworks that I shared, and read his own notes on his paintings: 'the new form, recognisable, yet inchoate, aspirant'.

I think of moons and suns, and of how we re-present ourselves time after time; I believe that there is only one point in our lives when we are rightly known or understood, and I have an unsentimental instinct that there is only one chance of fulfilment.

In his letter, Al talks of his 'unreserved' love for me, and of his inability to reconcile himself to the idea of a future together.

On the windowsill lies a small piece of tile. A corner is sheared off the tiny fragment of ceramic, the arm is modelled in colour, and there is an oblong window across the top, full of red and yellow fruit, like stained glass. It is a little sculpture of a pinball machine, that Seb made when he was fifteen. I look out across the sea, past the quince tree and the blue gate, past the hollyhock where my mother and father drank tea, and the tanned, adolescent boy mended his bike on the lawn, while, a mile away now, the recently-arrived Al prunes roses, weeds and scythes the long grass at the deserted family home.

At our reunion, his eyes had followed me, unblinking. In his tracksuit bottoms and lumberjack shirt, he was not playful or passionate or childlike: only tangled in fronds of doubt and ambivalence, seeking approval and escape. He sat on the sofa, with its cotton throw of flowery red and black design, and its faint emblems of fleur-de-lis on the faded Indian material, in exactly the way he had positioned himself to once ask, "What can I offer you?" and was moved to bewildered grief by my unhappiness.

"I found you were coming to terms with the situation between us better than I was. I was suffering because I wanted you to need to see me every weekend, and you were wanting to get on with your writing."

As he speaks, I glimpse a transitory truth, as in a diamond: a bright need on both sides, but unrelated and remote and brittly angry. As the jewel spins, I understand an inharmonious difference and change - there is bloody danger in mining here: I have been whooping over fool's gold as the seeming treasures trickled through my fingers. What has kept us together is the same misconception: we have both sought the benign reflection from the teasing diamond shard, clambering and shoving over the piles of detritus interminably, until the image smiles back unconditionally and for ever, and we are really loved at last.

"Well. What now? Make us a coffee, love. Is that alright?"

Fred has called to offer a more considered condolence.

"So what went wrong? Did you have no idea he was going to chuck you?"

He pats me on the shoulder, while looking at the pictures on my wall, his eyes screwed up.

"But why be surprised? It's the same thing, everywhere, don't you see? What happens to individuals is happening all over the world. It's fear, the sickness at the heart of things. Oh, the horror, my dear!"

He takes his cup, and rolls a cigarette.

"You look at these newsreels after any atrocity - see that sheer bloody incomprehension on the faces of the people lifting the stretchers? We can't do anything but stand on the sidelines and watch. Watch what the freaks do - the real freaks, Jo - not what you and I think we are. But we've helped to spawn them - we're all responsible. We create the enemy, and stand back terrified - we indulge all the tyrants and criminal organisations and multi-nationals and tinpot dictatorships, because it's easier than thinking for ourselves, and then we all become victims in the global neurosis."

"But Al isn't my enemy - he's here in the village and we're talking things over."

"You empowered him, though."

"Why would I?"

" Laziness."

"Laziness about what?"

"Your responsibility to yourself."

"And what's the cure for that?"

"Understanding it. Changing."

He drains his cup.

"I'll disappear, then, Jo - only checking that you're OK."

"Feel much better now, Fred. Thanks so much."

"Your apples will soon be ready for picking, kiddo."

"Not quite. I'll get some cartons from the shop. I'll save you some. I'll be glad when I've harvested them. I'm sick of kids scrumping every year - I haven't the energy for it this time."

I stroll across the promenade to the seashore to join Al: he wears a violet tee-shirt and shorts in the strong sunshine, and drapes his arm across my shoulder, as we pass children from the schools I teach in. They cover each other in sand and shout, "Hiya, Miss!" as Al tries to cup in his hands the two lavender butterflies which dart round his face, and leaps over small ox-bow pools in the grass near the beach. I think of Elvira Madigan, and her lover Sixten Sparre, eating berries and truffles in the woods, passing children playing blind man's buff, being dealt the black aces by a fortune teller, Sixten's wanting to see the world through his sweetheart's eyes - "Isn't that what love is?"- their love threatened as food and money ran out, and their suicide pact in a woodland glade: Elvira chasing butterflies, Sixten's killing her, and then himself.

Al's youthful skin is plumped and freckled; there are beads of sweat on his face and fair-skinned arm. I see how his eyebrows are slightly bleached, and once more, he appears numinous and irreproachable; blessed in some arcane way; his existence full of promise. I strain to combat the terror I feel at the passing of each moment of this summer, and at my own deepening tomb, real and deadly chill as the dark sandy burrows being dug by the teenagers behind me. As we walk onwards, arms round each other, the muddy runnels glitter in my sunglasses: everywhere is a pattern of ripples and shallow puddles: it is impossible to judge depths, distances, relationships, time. We walk and walk, passing a barnacled hulk of breakwater: we take off our sandals and shoes to step in the rivulets and refresh our feet as we go, and the sun shines still in our faces. By now we are a long way into the greyish mud-flats, famous for cockles and oyster-catchers. We look up to the far-off beach, and step out towards it. But the mud is blacker and more slimy between our toes, and as we jump from one apparent safe spot to another, we find we are mistaken, and lurch quickly to another, squelching deeper in the mire, clinging to one another and looking wildly round for a pathway.

"We'll retrace our steps, shall we?" I ask Al's whitely negating back, bent slightly in anxiety. He scrutinises the shifting sands beneath him.

"We should have gone back the way we came, ages ago."

He hesitates as I decide instead to take us forward quickly, and chance the deepening clayey channels, until we make the shore. We have come much further than we realised, traversing a black, stinking effluent now blocking us from safety and the glinting margin of mountains and sky in the welcoming distance inland, but, with mouths set, we persevere, until, after almost an hour, we sit light-heartedly again on pink shells and white stones, and can wash our feet in the clear rock pools of the shore. The sunshine is good, and the smooth pebbles and the limpid pools, and the sight of the hazy hills over our shoulders, where sheep graze and yellow broom buds, buzzed amid by bumblebees, where soft grasses wave, above the glistening shallow sea, where my father's ashes mingle yet with sons of sons of a plankton dynasty: invisible microbes insensible of their own earlier incarnations.

I remember Siddhartha's last battle with the self which had caused him so much pain, and how, when he found himself at the river, he recognised in its flowing movement the phenomenon of perpetual newness, and understood that we are reborn in every moment. He discovered how all the sights and sounds in the world were joined in one; how all the sufferings and pleasures were one; how together they formed the timeless and continuous stream of life - and he was finally able to surrender to this unity.

Siddhartha's philosophy is hard to live, but it occurs to me that I have already experienced the same dissolving of parameters, with what I naïvely describe as writer's eyes. I have seen how a thing seems to be a certain way only because of its relationship to other things, and when that dividing line melts away there are no separate existences, and no time.

I sense now that through art I can celebrate that simultaneity; that cohesion between all the things of the world; that infinite palimpsest. I could submit to that faculty of mine to perceive and create; I could let go of the quest for love, and stare instead in holiness of being at the sun, the butterflies, the sparkling sky, the eternity of landscape. So, shall I allow him to go, now?

Not yet....not just yet, as I pick up the shotgun from the pine needles on the ground.

There will be a lull of conversation, and trips to other shores, while the builders move in and my apples hang unplucked. There will be suggestions of love on the dole, and buying the beer kit, and cooking vegetable pies together.

There will be hand-in-hand strolls through the streets and

churchyards of northern towns flagged with gravestones, where the sun shines on laughing voices of other lovers behind the groomed yews, where moorland sweeps away from Blakean mills and blackened chimney-stacks.

Here we will eat toffee brittle filled with nut shards, from Asian shops where silk saris speckled with sequins hang in the bright prairie light of the industrial day, and little dresses with seamed hems and sleeves in turquoise and gold chiffon swing in rows in doorways, where deep rolls of velvet lie, and where rainbow-sequinned sandals covered in bells, with small heels and toe-rings are piled in Smiths Crisps cartons.

Here the shops, the dark jewellers' and the grocers', smell of armpits and curry and discarded leaves from the *Kama Sutra* and outside in the street the eyelashes of Muslim girls chewing gum shine like black skeins of polished thread: here all is politesse, dumb submission, dainty footwear and money-grubbing humility, quirky with decoration, dreary with ritual - a dislocation of time and tribes repositioned with a grubby British patina of bread, dripping, beer, and black pudding, stale yet tumescent with shish-kebabs, served in rank orifices by knackered genies of the rusty lamp.

And here, in his rented house where it has always been problematical for me to live, I draw pictures of Al on lined exercise-book paper, with felt-tips balanced on a plate, and Tippex and yellow highlighter - one portrait angelic, with smudged colours and young Roman virility, profound and sweet, and the other the teacher - tending earthwards; bespectacled and grizzled. And we buy art books, and read aloud the life of Klimt or Turner, pressing presents on one another in lieu of questions or answers, and walk in Wales again, with the sun setting even sooner these days, and we take to booking into hotels, as work begins in earnest on my home, and chatting to locals in pubs new to us, and we are a long way away from the days we threw apples across my lawn before he went to college, and where he put his arms around me and told our friends he loved this woman, and reassured me that we were a couple, and nothing would tear him away.

Off he goes to the school to marshal the sports and watch football in the evenings: to shine in the Christmas play and take up basketball; to develop his cooking skills and examine his wrinkles in the mirror, and have more money to spend, and learn to drive, and live the life of a man of thirty-one, at the beginning of his teaching career, with one eye upon a distant rosy cloud, where a high chair can be seen, and the thin voice of a new bride, piping welcome demands, can be faintly heard.

I stay at my mother's house, and give writing classes in the town where I grew up, take driving lessons myself, wait for the builder to make new my roof, my floors, my windows and doors, while dust and splinters drift down on the garden. No one shouts at the children stealing apples any more, and all the tiny mementoes are lying at the bottom of a cardboard carton like the one filled with glittering sandals in the northern town.

All the nights I lie in the attic at my mother's house, listening to the cry of seagulls.

Then one morning, on her way to the shops, she falls against the step.

She lies on a trolley in the hospital as Lottie and Charles and I peer at her: on her lips a faint brown crust has dried and we prop her against the pillows, until tomorrow.

"I'm sick of shocks," she says; by nature resistant to them and their threat of change and the horrid insistence that life is in flux; needing, since she was a girl, things to remain in place, to relax her guard and relish the world that interests her so. But it is always a house of cards: one's mother dies young; one's children cease to need one; no one eats end-of-the-month pie any more; one's husband grows old and ill and quiet; no one will go dancing: one's friends drop dead in the flowers; one's eyes fail; one's day is empty when one had known the bliss of tending babies and wheeling out the pram. One's grandchildren live far away and one's daughters choose incomprehensible avenues to walk and weep down.

Lottie and I take Charles to the parks and woods, and hinterland fields where we had once looked for tadpoles, refreshing our consciousness in the green shades of childhood, where we went to school. Here is the stone, worn smooth by our bottoms, on the wall where we'd sat in gangs: in the middle of this playground, Lottie and I had posed for the school photograph, sisters with sheepish smiles, in big ribbons and flannel skirts made from our dad's old trousers: Lottie sitting fat-legged on the teacher's upright chair, her shoulders and face round; her eyes trusting, heavy-lidded and unbruised: me alongside and leaning inwards in pretend protectiveness, my face stone-shaped, worn thin by spiteful ideas of how best to extinguish her. We find the corner shop where we spent pennies on lemonade crystals and black liquorice sticks; the open space where we played *Nyoka, the Jungle Queen*, at dinnertime, before our sitting; the gates where mothers waited at hometime - where a pram once contained my baby sister, where I was hoisted aboard, and given an ice-cream, and wheeled home to the peeling stained-glass window and pie.

"What's different between us is that I need and like companionship - a playmate and mentor - and you've always wanted reassurance," Lottie tells me, tucking her arm comfortably through her partner's, as they set off for their car.

I talk to Al next day on the phone: my mother will need someone with her while she recovers; I will certainly have to pass my test now; I'll find some work near by, for now.

We meet at my house, and I tell him of the school interview I've been offered.

"But if you think we could live together in Bury, I'll tell them I'm not interested - they can forget it."

"Finances would be a problem."

"They wouldn't have to be - I could do some supply teaching - I wouldn't expect you to maintain me."

I have seen and loved something unsullied and blithe in this man, which I have both envied and coveted. His escapes from responsibility for another, and his reluctances I understand, and the longing for life and happiness to be of the moment, unexamined: he has told me often and irritatedly that everything was alright with us until I wanted commitment and a future with him; that I should have left things as they were; that when he started to think, he was in trouble.

"I'll have to give it some time. I want to be able to answer you sensitively."

"There's nothing to it - you either want me with you or you don't."

He looks through the window, at a boy and girl hanging around at my gate.

"I have to admit it. The age thing is still a problem to me."

PARIAH

The Entwhistle kids are eyeing the last of the fruit.

"Don't move," I hiss to Al, as he sits facing me, against the light.

But the children seem to have caught a turn of his head, and scamper off.

I throw open the front door, to tiptoe barefoot down the garden path and away along the lane after the two. They are walking with their backs to me at a curve in the road, and it is here that I pounce on them, grabbing each by the shoulder.

"Don't you even think about pinching my apples," I storm.

"We weren't," says the boy.

"Yes, you were - I've seen you here before, running onto the lawn and trying to knock them down."

"We haven't - it wasn't us."

"Well - tell your little friends, then," I waver, letting go, as we are all startled by a banging on the window of a house opposite, and the furious appearance of their mottled father, now screaming at me not to lay another finger on his kids, or he'll have the police on me.

I return home, to the man's fading shouts, and Al's mortified welcome.

"That was a daft thing to do."

"Well, I'm fed up with it - I give the apples to anyone who wants them, when they're ready."

Presently a young policeman appears at the door.

"We seem to have a bit of a problem here, I'm afraid."

Mr Entwhistle, it appears, has lodged an immediate

complaint by phone: I am to accompany the constable to the station to make a statement; Al can wait outside. I am finger-printed - "One lot for us, one lot for Scotland Yard" - photographed holding a board with a number printed across it, and my tape-recorded statement of the incident is made at a table in a small interview room.

"The wife was the one who wanted to go ahead - I think he would have been alright about it when he'd cooled down," says the PC to me.

Al hangs about outside while I am under arrest.

"Can I help you?" the desk sergeant asks him, after an hour.

"I'm waiting for a friend to give a statement."

"What's the charge?"

"Assault."

"How long's he been in there?"

"It's a she, actually."

I am cautioned, in a polite interview with a detective inspector, and, brand sizzling, meander with my lover back to the house. I get my things together, picking up my mail from where the builder has left it, on a windowledge.

"Thanks for being with me, anyway."

"That's OK. I'm glad I was. But," - coquettishly - "we still haven't really resolved anything, have we?"

"Yes, I think we have."

I pull the door shut behind us.

"We must make a clean break."

"That's very tough of you, Johanna."

"You want a life: you want experiences of your own: you can't commit to me: you want to be free, don't you?"

I turn, forcing his eyes to look into mine. He lowers his glance.

"Yes, I suppose I do."

In silence we make our way past the brackenish valerian and the overgrown rockery. I remember how his loyalty has always been to that other, missionary, life: how it has almost destroyed me, in those Liverpool evenings with his college friends from whom I was banned, and in the weekends of his return, when he dined with the family, and I walked with him in the rain to the off-licence, where he bought cider for their meal, and I went home, under my brolly, to wait for him. Now I watch full-blown roses drop their petals as we brush by, and as we turn at the place where the gate used to hang: it is now lying among stones and brambles and fallen fruit; covered like everything else here in fine dust and sand.

Until now we have managed to sustain love of a kind, in an AI-inspired Eden filled with butterflies and unquestioning frolics. But, savage that I am, disregarding the silent and hypocritical rules of survival, I have ushered in reality, and stung his dreaming forces into deadly defence.

We stand together in the road outside and look back at my cottage.

"Say goodbye to all that, Al - this will probably be the last time you see it."

"Oh, I hope not - I still love you, you know...in fact, I'm head over heels in love with you...I want us to be friends, at least, Johanna - our lives are inextricably entwined...I want to cook curries for you...I want us to stay at hotels...I want to come and see you here...and send you presents...I can't really take this in, you know - I didn't want this. Why has it got to be like this?"

He knows why, and presses me thus feebly no further.

I idly imagine the scenes from this point, as if on a storyboard of my own design: dully, I recount to myself the substance of the narrative of our affair - the family has gone now; there is no need for him to visit this place. In the future, he will find an excuse for this idiosyncratic choice - like old art school friends, now resplendently bourgeois, who once walked barefoot and drank pints of beer with me. He will be smoothly reinstated in the bosom of the family, or unite with someone more appropriate, of whom his mother and father, in matching white topis, must approve.

We catch the train from which I will alight at my childhood hometown, and upon which he will continue to Bury.

In the carriage, I regard the young man sitting across from me.

Three years ago, I sat at a party, next to this person whom I hardly knew and hardly noticed. We had exchanged a few remarks, and, in a twinkling, this lad in shorts, not worth a second look to me at that time, had taken on a life of his own, like Pinocchio! But I had been the puppeteer! I had breathed into the little wooden fellow the life I needed to respect! I had Jiminy Cricketed him to power! I had handed over the gun so he could deliver the annihilating bullet into my heart! It was I who had oiled smooth movement into that creaking patella, and choreographed the awkward wave into something operatic and transcendental: I who had made a ballet of a limp step sideward, and found poised languor in a gauche fall of the wrist.

As I watch him, Al's features grow coarse and rough-hewn, and his smile fades into something stiff and fixed: his voice falls to a mechanical drone: his attitude, as I lean to kiss him goodbye, becomes that of the sedentary boozer before his glass, gazing nowhere. And instead of sadness and sorrow, I am suffused with revulsion at his cowardice; nauseated that I have been forced to take the full and congealing responsibility for the decision to finish. I have clutched too desperately at the dolly mixtures of youth and domestic bliss, and have excused his lack in my avarice for the idyll: I have merely been a middle-aged woman in a dreadful aspic of longing and regret. It has been more pressing to have the tall, amusing, but immature and ambivalent young man in my life, than to recognise its futility, and I have let yearning for validation by him eclipse the facts.

I draw a line through this interminable tragicomedy: I decide to give form to the inchoate stuff of my life.

As I descend from the train, I hear a distant drumming sound and the loud splintering of glass inside my head, and my brain is dazzled for a moment by a hail of rainbow fragments, of colours I have never imagined: purple-blues and yellow-reds and synthetic brilliant pinks shudder and fade, synthesized into a far-off tribal chant.

The neat train and the wooden white man disappear.

So I turn, and I walk again to my mother's house along the

shore, treading on pebbles of white, grey and rosy brown, picking up one or two to examine the threads of black and blue sandwiched between their worn layers, finding large cankered shells of pearl and ochre, fanning into brittle laminates, glowing with soft mother-of-pearl and silver-gold. Small marbly-pink stones nestle by accident in the bowl of one, as if they've found their home, as happy and determined as a bluff seed of dandelion stuck on a hawthorn, in rude ecstasy of arrival and impudence of rebellion.

I sit on the beach and pull out a sketchbook. In front of me lie many mixed smooth stones: hard jasper and slatey cool blues are also drying in the coolish air after the ebbing waves. Slimy green lichenous seaweeds cling to the base of the nearby promenade wall, and I draw a picture of a slabby, craggy boulder as I think of what I have just done. I am already missing him, as I dip a brush in a tin can I've filled with seawater.

The sea crawls in ripples a few feet away from me, leaving a stain on the white sand: a woman and little girl come down onto the shore, and the mother leans to pick up a stone for her daughter, who wears a coat too big for her: she reminds her the sea won't harm her; it's only water.

And already Al is miles away, heading towards his mark-books and his rites of passage, as I stand up and put my pencils and brushes in their box and make my way to my mother's, passing by the railings on the prom, and looking down at the surface of the sea. I see black shoals of silver whitebait which leap up and flick brightly in the still air, and jellyfish open and close as they have for aeons.

"You've got a class tonight," my mam reminds me, as I enter her kitchen.

My mother sits at the window of her flat, choosing a selection from her catalogue of Talking Books, wearing a blue taffeta-silky top and a flowered skirt, while the cleaning lady vacuums.

Tonight I will sit among the dozen writers gathered for my

help. I will watch them arriving and arranging themselves; I will wonder what Al will be doing , and think that he has never known anything of my life as a writing teacher, yet I am osmotically familiar with every detail of his working day, from the befringed maths teacher's giant cleavage to the fridge where the Friday cheese and wine is saved, to the end-of-term dreadlocks of Molly Pratt. I know when babies are due, when nervous breakdowns are imminent, when inspections loom. I know how to pronounce the name of every Muslim child in his Year Three: I know who is applying for head of department posts and where.

He has no inkling of the claustrophobia of this drawing-room, in the town where I grew up and went to school: I haven't told him of the Dutch woman's autobiography; the eighty-eight year-old's Dickensian love story; the golfer's piece on the processional caterpillar; the retired accountant's potted local histories; the hairdresser's fulsome morality tales. He knows nothing of what goes on in this room, where logs burn and sometimes fall onto the thick carpet; where for hours they politely listen and privately judge, and I guide and praise, and where once I blurt out that *relationship* is what it's all about - and know myself a savage.

Their crafted pieces have their place in the monthly mags, but I find that I want iconoclasm, to cliché-bust, to trailblaze. My urge is to shake out the distracting details of their work, and find and show what they are really saying with the caterpillar and the chronicle: what they really wonder at and long to examine. So, during the public reading of the Dutch woman's drama, I am astounded at her desk-top delivery of the icily-poignant moment when her husband leaves her for his secretary - she shows us a world of furs and glass-doored buildings, ham shanks for soups for the in-laws, hairdos and high Amsterdam society, wherein she was reduced to humiliation, and from which she has created a new life for herself; taking the ferry to England alone, finding a home in Wales, joining this writing class, and sitting here in a crisp pink jacket by the fire, to tell these strangers how it came to pass. I want more of it, and to give power to the Dutch elbow, despite: "It is not necessary for me to publish my writing: I am telling my story, and I do it just for me!"

And a pastoral moon sails by the far window of the detached house where we sit in a circle under the roof and under the stars, and from where in front we can see a panoramic sky and sea: I try to memorise the colours in the chord of chat: I encapsulate three moods in a triptych - in the centre, pink bundled clouds catapult and bounce to the low horizon, reflected in the water like bon-bons, and shining back from rosy pools on the rich brown sands: to the left, a hot sudden sunset behind the local blackening hills; on the right, a distant coastline underneath thin swathes of cloud and shell-blue stretching skies, and nearer to us, other windows catching the last brands of sun. I want to tell them that in these juxtapositions lies a secret: that form lies in seeming formlessness; that only in ever-changingness will security be achieved; and the same truth in language and story-telling will be discovered only by experiment and the greedy and curious creation of new patterns; it must all be a forging ahead and a making anew, in every moment: and as light turns to shade even here, and as the heat of day recedes into cool night, the planet spins: and we will not fall off it, and there will always be sun and sky and sea and moon, always in relation to one another, and that relation will always be threatened by suggestion and possibility, yet always stay fast, despite the perpetual urge to break away, the umbilical of love and freedom, and life and death, ticking always side by side in eternity.

I pick up a poem that a girl called Ellen has written, where she describes red berries against green hawthorn. Yes, I've seen it myself, Ellen, and have boasted, as well, about the red seeming redder because it is in relation to the green: it, in turn, manifesting more verdantly, and, in general, things presenting themselves as more or less of what they are because of what they exist in relation to...so Ellen is a great poet in relation to Otto, and I am a small one in relation to Daniel, and Reuben, perhaps, great, in relation to Eve... and the lanes of hawthorn and yarrow run ahead of us, long and full of seasons, where we cast small or great shadows.

There is no time any longer for mooning: what is becoming important now is a poetic truth: that we are somehow kept going: our hearts pump and the blood carries oxygen to our extremities in a solid bridging rhythm, and life can begin again in each moment; and that moment contains all of life, and nature lies before us and provides us with beauty, and I am reassured of that, each time I take a stroll in the parks or glens of my childhood. Between the boulders I sketch in the streams, I witness a triangle of water which no one has ever seen or will ever see again - not this triangle, at this time in history, in this light and in my mood. During the experience I sense a blessing, and I note it to myself amid all the dapplings, and a leaf hanging by a thread, spinning, as everyone has seen it, in slanting September sunshine.

As I button my raincoat for supply teaching work in school again, I know my thumb pressing on the light brown moulded plastic roundness: I am familiar with its four little holes where beige cotton binds it to its mother garment; and I don't like this mac yet I wear it incessantly, like the checked skirt with fishy panels and the amorphous jumpers to hide in, for taking the registers in those rooms where, with fan heaters humming, I try to understand Welsh cartoon stories and answer questions on William of Normandy, and help children draw maps of Great Britain.

And off into the night, to creep upstairs quietly, past my sleeping mother, to check her painting of a row of cottages under the moon, to leave her an encouraging note about it, to climb higher to my own room, where I switch on the bedside light and am dazzled by the red and yellow of two roses in a thin vase, which I look at through a heart-shape I make with my hands, before I undress in the dark, thinking that I should paint a picture of it there and then in the imprecation of that bright light. I believe sleepily that colour and time are tied up in fluid eternity, as I climb into my attic bed, and listen to the seagulls on the roof, and blink with my writer's eyes at our own moon, waxing at the middle of September: and I will find that peace of Siddhartha when I take up my paints again.

And here is Fred, on a sunny morning, come to a nearby garage to buy a part for his secondhand Mini.

"That bit of yellow works and it stays back - you know why? Because of that purple you've used there," he says to my mother.

"I like that," about a painting of mine hanging in the hallway, of two straw-hatted girls, whose arms are specked with white paint, where I'd packed it up with another picture before it was dry.

Fred has a cup of tea with us in the kitchen, and talks about his car.

"They're in stitches, these dealer guys, because I don't care that it's a collector's piece - I just like it; it was only three hundred quid and it reminds me of that film... anyway, it broke down, and I was taking some of my steamships to Leeds, to Ronnie, and I had to ring him up, and there was a woman from America there waiting for my stuff, and he had to pay for her to stay overnight in a hotel. You - you never come to see me, Johanna. I keep thinking of things I want to tell you, and I'm going to ring you up, but I don't want to be rejected."

"Don't be daft, Fred. I'm trying to write."

"Yes, yes, I know. I know. I know. Have you heard from lover-boy?"

"No."

"So now what?"

"Just get on with things."

"You might find that ordinary life is not so bad."

"What do you mean?"

"I mean living in the way you've been afraid of for so long. You'll get more satisfaction from that."

"I know."

"No, Jo. It's easy to get immobilised by love, but when it doesn't work out, it's the attitude you then take that makes the real difference - you know, that old Zen thing about doing whatever it is you have to do wholeheartedly, even the dishes."

"I feel a bit of a fool, now."

"No, I'm not saying you're foolish. I understand, because

I'm the world expert in self-delusion. It's not important how you've lived. But where has it got you? You're just here, on this doorstep, with no perfect life or perfect love, and it's the same for everyone you've ever met or loved or known - nobody's got a clue. I bet none of those friends you made abroad had got it sorted out? Peace has to come from inside *you*. Love isn't the answer, Jo - not that kind, anyway."

He sniffs my mam's lavender bush.

"Get on with your work, now, and throw away those bloody diaries."

"I'll see you soon, Fred."

He puts his arm round me.

"Not very firm."

"Oh, I'm sorry!"

"No! No! Not you - the arrangement - not a very firm one."

I wonder at Al's silence, and the time passing - a fatty, stringy casing around and begetting our actions, like a membrane or a caul.

The tides are high, with the waves bringing up great grey rocks and dropping them on the promenade so it has to be closed off, and I see people walking along, among the rocky litter in the sunshine.

I watch those scenes through the window of the car I am learning to drive in, and I use my sketchbook to try to remember what to do at roundabouts. For hours I study the Highway Code, and discover a dull beauty in the mix of yellow lines and possible trespass of them, and a short constabulary thrill in the recognition of the triangular red of warning signs, mollifying myself with the friendly blue-calm of information signs, unthreatening, matter-of-fact yet, again, not to be trifled with in possible future need for evidence and identity and placement: a potential c.v. ingredient, each one. I must wake up to its *gravitas*, and I do, and I pass the test, by driving confidently at thirty where it is allowed, and forty, even, with the examiner telling me that his wife is a teacher, too, who 'learns' children with problems.

I have heard nothing from Al. I am numbed by the ruthlessness of my own thunging blood and by the slippery ease of his escape into marking exercise books and another year's membership of the gym. And I dodge the spray from the sea on my way to a new writing class.

On the prom is a rusting-up telephone where pound coins are stuck in the slot. I manage to push one in with a pencil, and I speak to Frank on his fifty-ninth birthday.

My mam makes dinners for me, and waits for her magnifying glass from the hospital, and I promise that soon I will buy a car and take her into the country, and she can come and stay in my house when it is ready, and warm her back against the radiators.

I turn down the job: I wait again for teaching work: and there are many newly redundant teachers waiting for the same work, too.

I will have to go to the bank again.

BUDDHA

While Lottie irons, I sit painting in the hearth, and chat to Juliet, in the farmhouse under Snowdon.

"I want to get the feeling of the landscape, roughly representing what's there, but using different colours from the actual ones. Instead of those dirty greens," - pointing at the scrubby meadows falling from the house - "I might use a violet, next to a hot yellow, like this one, and with the brushstrokes and the varying density of paint and the new relationships that are created, still capture its particular quality. It's really all about colour and what it can do... how emotion can be expressed, not only by means of the 'real' greens and browns of the hills and hollows, but also in the way the colour is mixed and placed ...do you see what I'm getting at?"

I work from photographs on my mother's kitchen table: from the pictures I took on Anglesey, while Seb surfed and snorkelled. I sit anew on the cold stones, sensing my way through the damp green seaweeds on the bouldered beach; hearing the crack and suck of the barnacles clinging to the host, watching the waving corn of a cliff field, where a red windmill stands above the curved fissures of machine tracks, that scoop round and down in the summer meadow.

In the Welsh hills of autumn I walk with Charles and Lottie, scrambling over scree towards the groups of rocks I snap with my camera, for later, when, in acrylics, plastic washes in violet blues and putty-coloured greys will give the Cader Idris slopes under its new vermilion horizon a sense of the Australian outback: aboriginal, potent, impregnated with myth and elemental rhythms.

The reds and golds: the berries of the winter haw, still pendent from a branch Lottie has stuck in a pot on a tawny-iron table in her makeshift garden, whisper something more than beauty of nature: there is a call to me in that glowing rich hue: an immanence which spells something other than fullness of the normal spectrum - a scintillating energy is contained in the tints themselves; in their atomic purity and in the softening and sullying of this by particles of dust and pollen and disintegrating sheepshit even, rising into the ionosphere with psalms of decay, giving the lie to what is before us: illustrating only and forever the maya of the horizon; the hip-hop of relativity in the hawthorn berry and its twig, where colour itself holds a secret of life: as long ago splashes, drifting blues and reds from the stained-glass paper, falling from the window on my sister's pram cover had been mesmerising in themselves, as well as in faery celebration of the babe, and of the criminal sibling who leaned in on her.

As I had then jerked down the pram handle to slither the infant forth, now I force pen, crayon or brush in and around, through the defining natural outline, to shake up the formula, impose a new arrangement upon it, aiming speculatively, prayerfully, at cohesion and celebration: sometimes succeeding, sometimes not.

Back home, from my window, I see the framed scene of the horse chestnut I have watched as it changes, year after year, standing silently in the rain, verging now into smears of ochre and dense passages of blue-green shadow. Coming at me, through the open frame, the leaf-shapes and clumped sprays spread in perfect equilibrium. I sense the pulsating life within, of squirrels dancing from twig to light branch, and of the yellowing point of quitting, when a leaf spirals down in speed and spinning lassitude, unnoticed, yet bright as the sun. The scene begins to press itself more urgently upon my vision, entering me with luminous power, taking me back to its mass of cell, chlorophyll, tannin, bark, splinters, lichens - the dusty abundance, where light spatters through in glimmering silver strokes, and the breeze lifts and runs and cools my vision in its coursing back and forth.

In my house I paint vases of roses: the room smells of detergent, like the Reading flat my mam had found for us, when Seb was a baby in his pink carry-cot. I see again the bulky sofa where I cradled him, while Frank drew me, in the careful, measured English style we'd been taught, in the tradition of Sickert and Coldstream, in the placing of a pencilled mark, the measuring fore and aft of the point, the delicate, tentative connection to determine the next, and on through a web of fine lines to suggest the figure, then the figure in context - the correspondence between these dots a testimony only to a withering aesthetic which was dying on the vine even then; I look at the face of the young mother as she breast-feeds her baby; at her short-sleeved black jersey; her arms over-plumped from the misjudged markers; her gaze programmed by the Royal Academy: civilised; feminine; wifely; moon to man's sun.

"I have to respect the person who created the painting or the sculpture before I can admire the work of art itself," - now I see how dependent and romantic was that utterance, and how I had needed everyone to be avatar or saint, so that I, too, could be delineated and defined in the stardust falling from the master's breath, brush or chisel.

But a work of art is no moral measure of the artist, and the artist nature is not lovable, anyway, because of its intensity, its estrangement from the norm, its amorality and asociality, its relentless truth-seeking.

A starchy postcard comes from Al: he requests the return of the Marcus Aurelius, and the William Golding. He has been seeing someone from his old college ever since we split up. He has heard from, and has arranged to meet, the Greek girl, no longer married. I phone him: "And how do you feel about children and your rites of passage now?"

"Oh, I don't think I'll be bothering with any of that."

Through the window of the library, I watch the dusk fall over the Conwy river this autumn evening, waiting for my writing students, remembering how Frank and I dug for bait here and cooked mussels in seawater in tin cans over a beach fire, in our student summers. We hawked his oil painting of the castle around the pubs, but there were no takers, and eventually it was used for something else or destroyed.

Now I pick a book from the shelves: *Who's Who in British Art*.

There is Frank, 'Godfrey, Frank. Born 1936. Married Ruth Godfrey. Three sons.'

Then in comes my first student, with her life story typed out on a sheaf of paper, tucked casually into a briefcase. While she reads her excerpts aloud, I examine my reaction. I have never been told - but what does it matter if Frank has re-married and not let me know, when they've lived together for years, and have a son? I have only the nagging sense of having kept faith with some tacit, misunderstood pact.

The woman reads from her sheets, her voice clogged with emotion at the account of the visit from her estranged husband: how changed she is, and he's noticed, and is unnerved. She revels in her own majesty and his confusion: still in thrall to him, despite her affirmation of her own triumph of progress in moving on.

I am weary: her words float down through the bookish air: I smile and tell her what is good and bad, in my opinion, about the piece. As she sulks, the motes settle on the table and upon my opened file, with its scribbled plan for this evening. Another student casts a critical glance at this chaos.

"If I'd been doing this class, I would have planned the lesson clearly and had lists of the subjects I was going to deal with each week."

We pack away and I look out at the quayside, and at the dimly elegant masts of a sailing ship, hovering only yards from my face in the night. Light reflects from the gloss of wood lacquer and the broad deck, as the hull of the empty vessel tilts towards me, its sails languishing in pale linen loops, blown limply by the wind, and casting moving shadows, among which, in the patchy lamplight spilling on the quayside, I see Al. He is standing there, a cigarette in his hand, lifting his crooked arm to his mouth and back again, his head moving stiffly at a slight angle from left to right, in a robotic motion, his glasses glinting as he stares in my direction. He is wearing a tee-shirt, just as he did in the summer, as he leaned against my garden wall, talking to my neighbours. I focus my gaze and know this must be a trick of the light, but I want the image to remain: there is something shocking but revelatory here: I am able to assess him unrestrainedly; to summon him up almost at will: to dwell on my reaction to this epiphany in cotton sleeves, whose face is turned to me in vulnerability and youth.

I see, as I look into his gaze, superimposed on the granite-slabbed harbour where I unravelled seaweed from paternosters with my husband-to-be, the untutored boy: his easy movements emphasising only his eager trust in me. And at last I know that it was not Al's love wherein I had sought redemption, but this very youthfulness. Seeing him, fixed in dappled, damp air, breathing and not breathing, the half-known truth which has floated in and out of my consciousness for so long takes form at last, impeccably and terribly: the younger the man, the keener the illusion of starting afresh, and living the reciprocal life, with a history to build, which can now never be. I know now that Al has not been a man I have loved, but a chance I have chased to become that Liverpool wife again, to construct my story anew and expunge my bitter remorse at taking away my son from his father.

For too long I have systematically milked the need to be seen as good in the eyes of the 'powerful', never having the motivation or courage to give authorship to my acts and volitions: things 'happened' to me, and I stood by, separate from them, protesting my innocence of them, by passive resistance to them. I have denied responsibility, both for my adult acts and for the creative urge to experiment, which was stamped in me at conception. Hence the imbalance, the eagerness to stay in submission to the will of another, to be the reflector, the verifier, the passive lunar affirmation of the most sunlit parts of another - man, artist, parent or lover. And hence the difficulty of admitting the irrepressible compulsion to artistic and human authenticity. I see so clearly now that I have gained many advantages from my silvery position: it has been vastly in my interest for my faint light to be so easily clouded over, and to sustain the blameless liberty of the wronged: I have become as fascinated by the benefits of being a victim as I was by the shards of light through my tears, when I stood on a chair as a child and cried, and I now discern the payoffs of my hidden, subconscious, agenda.

I have been responsible for all the events of my life: it has all been my own choice. Things were so much easier to accommodate, when they were not my fault: if I 'had to' give up my study of art; if I 'had to' get married; if I 'had to' leave my husband; if my life had not been of my making. But I was the one who had reneged on my creative life, who had deprived my son of his father, and drawn sentimental succour from what might have been. Whatever the circumstances, it was by my hand that our lives - all three - had irrevocably altered.

I know that I have made an insoluble drama of my pains in the chase for love, but I begin to acknowledge that as I suffered, so I experimented. As I screwed my tear-filled eyes up to the light and became entranced by its rainbows, so I have studied and processed the colours and contrasts of my experiences. But within the wavering flame of the self, the creative nature, too, has been in danger - and I know that not until I begin to take responsibility for the actions of the self will the artist also find peace. So I cannot continue in this debilitating investment in another, with its dividend of approval and eternity of dependency, any more than I could have gone on in my compulsive, adrenalin-charged newspaper work.

The moment has arrived - the amber of guilt has formed into a clasp at last; the neurosis has sucked all nourishment from me; the poisoned leaf can fall - and the agent of this change has not been the explosive and uncontingent eureka! I'd hoped for, but the whimper of my own analysis and weariness, the love and need of beauty and balance: the new and greater shock of awareness of what has gone and what is left to me, overlaying and replacing my fading misconceptions.

I put up a hand to the clear pane: the image is gone, and I

hear only a soft glassy tinkle in the rigging.

Lights are switched off one by one, as my students move for the door.

In London, in discussion of the reception planned after his big retrospective exhibition in Liverpool, Frank asks Seb if it would be my sort of thing. I reply that it would. Seb is to travel up with Frank's first-born, Paul: I am to arrange a lift with Seb's friend, and meet them all there.

From my mother's kitchen I take details, on an envelope spotted with butter, of where to meet Mo. Behind me, the cleaning-lady is telling us of a newly-opened shop nearby, where it is possible to buy no end of cheap goods.

"They give you a bag, too," she says, as she moves a rug listlessly over the faint stains of spilled tea on the linoleum.

I leave them, in desultory discussion of car boot sales and funerals, to change into my retrospective getup. It doesn't look the way it did in the Chester store any more: there, with the back and side-view mirrors and the silver tongue of the assistant, I managed to kid myself I was imbued with underplayed *savoir-faire* - now all that is reflected is a fifty-two-year-old teacher in a skimpy suit, off to a union meeting.

On my way to find Mo, on a business enterprise scheme somewhere in the town, I look in at the bargain shop, as instructed. There, among imported gadgetry and mass-produced ornaments, I pick up a sketchbook, opening it to touch the cheap, rough, straw-flecked greyish paper, which reminds me of that cocooned drawing time, when crayoned princesses nested in tulle.

At four o'clock, at an office, I lean over the counter to wave for attention from the receptionist.

"Coming - coming...who are you looking for?"

"Mo Chapman."

"Is it important?"

"He's giving me a lift to an exhibition in Liverpool."

"What - painting?"

"Yes."

"Oh, I like painting. I like scenes."

"It's not like that - it's more, um, abstract."

"Oh, I don't understand that stuff - can you tell me what it's supposed to be about?"

Outside the gallery I climb out of Mo's van, in my painful high-heels, and lean on it while he puts my coat into the boot. He munches on a meat paste roll, as I look up from the cobbled boulevard. Above me a banner waves in the wind. Upon it is inscribed the autograph of Frank; the same signature which I've known on letters and inside painting and poetry books for thirty-four years: the hand which had penned the line: 'Were ever two souls so congruous?'

We enter: I excuse myself, to comb my hair in the marbled, Victorian Ladies room, already filling with Liverpudlian councillors and powdered and wigged dames of the city. A woman introduces herself as Linda, and, on discovering my relation to the great man, drags her friend across to meet me, and announces, despite my denials: "This is his wife!"

Then I find Mo again, and we climb the wide, spiral staircase: Seb arrives with his half-brother, seeming relaxed, and hugs me, with a joke about my outfit, then looks round for his father, while I wander among the torsos and busts I'd admired, uncomprehendingly, as a Wrexham student.

The gallery doors upstairs are being opened: there are glimpses of the work I saw last summer at Diorama, and as I crane, friends from Wrexham and Liverpool days pass me: some unrecognising; others, like the Beatle brother, grinning in surprise, as the crowds flow through and individuals separate themselves to make closer study of the drawings, or to examine the painter's brushwork.

Someone far ahead begins to speak, and a hush falls across the room.

The man speaks of Frank Godfrey's connection with Liverpool, of his influence on the city, and of the illustriousness of this show, spanning the twenty years since he left, and including award-winning photo-realist pieces from the preceding period.

Critics and collectors stand to attention: in my high-heels and crêpe suit I look ahead at the speaker, then become aware of Frank himself, standing a foot away, with his back to me, in jacket and trousers of a fluid, subtle woollen fabric.

Holding his hand, wearing his father's black felt hat, is Martin, and on the other side of the child stands Ruth, in a cool blue dress, her short blonde hair cut even and glossy.

Frank's massive paintings hang from the walls of three rooms: I know some of the works, but have never seen them in sequence like this before: his whole *oeuvre*.

More than thirty years have passed since we lived together in this city, in the rat-infested flat, deep in financial trouble. In a trice, it disappears: there is no paraffin spilling from the can onto the floor, no rag to wipe it up with and thence my fumy knees. Gone is the day the bailiff came and, across our breakfast, demanded Frank pay the arrears from his maintenance payments to Paul's mother.

"I haven't got any money."

"Has your wife, Mr Godfrey?"

"No."

"Empty your pockets, sir."

Gone is the Frank who placed on the table the mature equivalent of penknife, conkers and bits of string, and was summarily escorted to Walton Jail, and gone the self and baby, who sat amid the Saturday morning debris and the wrecked plans to visit the grandparents.

Where are these events? Where is the day he hurried down to this very gallery at the last minute, to enter the piece which would win first prize in the sculpture competition?

I look again at the back of the head of the famous painter, in his sixtieth year, standing in expensive clothes in front of me. What palimpsest is this? What parallel universe? What wife now, and what blond infant?

These paintings which surround me, in their 'psychic automism', large fleshy pictures of nude women and swarthy iconographic men, were made over the last two decades: since my departure from his life, and despite and during another domestic ensemble.

But the years were the same length for us all: there was no extra dimension where art could be produced: it was my world, too, wherein Frank chose to commit himself to his vocation and give it space and time: and where he found his voice.

Yet, as I watch a video being played to accompany the show, I know too that this is the young man I fished with in the Conwy estuary - and there is a newspaper picture of him, aged twenty-eight, holding the winning cheque from the sculpture contest.

In the film, Frank speaks of his philosophy and his development and influences; interspersed are still photographs of his mother and father and the sister who died early, a drawing of me, with Seb in my arms; the steelworks home of his parents, where they reared Paul.

The speech ends, and Frank turns and catches sight of me, as our son hands me a glass of wine.

Greetings and introductions are made: it seems impossible to express my pleasure in his success, but for a moment we look at each other and I manage to say, "Well done! Your mam and dad would be very happy!" before the crowd moves in again and the hubbub sets up.

There is a meal, a club, dancing and talking late into the Liverpool evening smelling of river and sea, where ships hoot in the Mersey air, and where my husband of youth celebrates his entry to the art establishment, and the scissors snip the cotton danglers from my psyche, clearing the picture forever of its long-time irritants and distractors.

The next day the two grown-up sons drive back to London, and I take the train alone, to the Welsh coast.

Walking up from the station, I am aware of the traces of late snow still lying in crannies on the mountains, and the downstream torrent of the brown spring river, hung over by bursting twigs on the black trees. It is dusk, and a new moon shows through the sighing reach of cloud: there is no white in the box of colours, but

I will be content to paint pictures from the blues and browns which remain.

At my cottage gate, I look into my garden to find clumps of gleaming, freshly-planted daffodils - Lottie has driven over, with a haul of bushes and flowering shrubs from her own lost gardens.

In the scattered mail on the hall floor is a notice about the imminent opening of the medium-secure unit, full of slick drawings and phrases to convince the fearful or sceptical: the patients are regarded as 'not an immediate threat to themselves or the community', and will be hemmed in by 'overhanging eaves and lightweight guttering' which 'cannot be climbed on'.

The menace will be contained and incorporated: there is nothing that cannot be accomplished to achieve those ends of denial and refusal: no panic that cannot be remodelled into smiling façades without dangerous eaves: no murderous impulse or flash of mad spirit which cannot be civilised by 'high, flat and tightly meshed security fences'.

It is completely silent in my home: on the windowledge stands the vase of silk flowers which Mary admired, and over the sofa is thrown the Indian cotton cover of red and black design.

I sit there to open a letter from Juliet. She has included a blurred picture of the scan of the new foetus, with its indistinct suggestion of impudent alienation, sealed away in a bright, numbered sac, insisting on its being with each tick of its mother's heart.

No one knew what to do with me when I announced my pregnancy, at five months. I watched myself expand as I sketched and wrote poems in Derbyshire in my pigtails, while my family tried to decide what would be best.

This new baby, with perfect nostrils and lips, with palpitating fontanelle, with holy fleshly submission to the world, will be born, as subject to the anxieties of its mother, emerging as puzzled and doubtful. And on and on the round will go: a small child will again gaze out to sea in a fat, serious way, while sibling and playmates frolic bare-legged in sandals amid the little waving flags on their crumbling sandcastles in the bright wind.

I look down the garden path, past my sister's primroses and the narcissus growing through the dirt. I glimpse the place where the maidenhair once flourished; there is nothing left of that, in the dark, freshly-appropriated soil. But, in my imagination, lit up as though by a torch-beam in an attic, I see it as vividly as in reality: its dense clumps of heraldic foliage a dull, powdery blue-green, and, after rain or dew, prisms crystallising delicately on the fine, bending leaf-planes, shooting spears of electric blues, greens and rose-red in the sunshine.

There comes another call for school: I pick up my bags, and set off for my mother's once more.

From the school built on a hillside where I sledged as a child, I look down over the village where she lives, and across the sea. It is hailing, and I can see from the heated schoolroom that tiny room, where I sleep sometimes, where seagulls cry high above as I dress, landing to squawk and stomp about on the flat roof.

Clouds edged with blue-grey hurry and change by the second, while my mother, vulnerable now and needy herself, pulls up her pearly satin nightdress to release the smells of bed and her body, and rubs ointment into her swollen knees, whose skin shines unnaturally as it stretches over the crumpled blue veins.

Across the school playing fields beneath me, lie roofs of red, slate-grey and black, with the same mercurial sheen as on my first Christmas mornings, now slanted under sun and March clouds. I can see the church across the road from my mam's flat, where I had unwillingly read the lesson on Sundays, and then the Sunday school building, where, standing on the parquet floors, in white cotton socks whose tops refused to grip, but hung baggily over the Clarks shoes my dad had polished, I quavered, 'There is a green hill far away', and 'Over the sea there are little brown children', from a hanging yellowing scroll I imagined had been donated by the missionaries.

And beyond the village where I lived as a child, and where I rocked my baby sister in the black pram, I see the beach, where we played in the summer and where our dad taught us to swim in the brown and blue breakers, now quietly fringing the full ocean, a palimpsest itself, stretching out to Ireland and America, receiving no new impression for long, offering no answer or guidance, only the spring tides, beyond the roofs and spires, surging to the farthest shores.